Ripped at the Seams

How Not to Spend Your Senior Year

BY CAMERON DOKEY

Royally Jacked

BY NIKI BURNHAM

Ripped at the Seams

BY NANCY KRULIK

Ripped at the Seams

NANCY KRULIK

Simon Pulse
New York London Toronto Sydney

First Simon Pulse edition June 2004
Copyright © 2004 by Nancy Krulik

SIMON PULSE
An imprint of Simon & Schuster
Children's Publishing Division
1230 Avenue of the Americas
New York, NY 10020

Designed by Ann Sullivan
The text of this book was set in Garamond 3.

Manufactured in the United States of America
10 9 8 7 6

Library of Congress Control Number 2003112912
ISBN-13: 978-0-689-86771-2
ISBN-10: 0-689-86771-9

For Danny

Ripped at the Seams

One

"I was abducted by aliens!"

Sami Granger's eyes flew open as the gray-haired woman in the lavender coat leaped in front of her and shouted tales of alien abduction right in her face.

"It's true, I tell you. They just swept me up into their force field and carried me into their spaceship. And once they had me on board, well, let me assure you . . ."

Sami looked into the woman's eyes. They were flying around her face, unfocused, *crazed*. Her hair was wild, too, tied in a bun in the back but teased into a high beehive on the top of her head. And from the smell of her, it seemed she hadn't bathed in a while.

The girl clutched her suitcase a little tighter and walked toward the exit. She picked up her step and tried to lose the woman behind one of the pillars that dotted the main hall at Port Authority Bus Terminal. But the deranged woman picked up her pace to match Sami's and continued her tirade as they walked. "I was scared at first, of course. But I have to admit, once they started the examination, I calmed down. Aliens have a gentle touch—certainly more gentle than the doctors at that hospital I was a prisoner in."

Sami had no doubt what kind of hospital this woman meant. Probably that Bellevue Hospital mental ward her father had warned her about. "They let the crazies out during the day," her dad had told her. "They take over the city. And then—if they can find their way back to the hospital—they crawl into their straitjackets at night."

At the time, Sami had figured that was just another of her father's arguments against her going to New York. But listening to the woman next to her drone on and on, Mr. Granger's tale of terror took on a sort of plausibility.

She tried to turn her attention from the babbling woman, hoping that maybe, if she completely ignored her, the woman would just go away and tell her tale to some other unsuspecting person. So Sami stared straight ahead and focused on the group of girls in front of her.

"I couldn't eat another bite. I'm completely full," Sami heard one of them say loudly.

"Oh, come on, you have to share this with me. My mother said I had to eat something for breakfast, but I can't possibly finish a whole apple," her friend pleaded.

"How are you supposed to dance on a full stomach?" the third girl in the trio asked.

"I know. That's why I need you two to share this with me."

The three girls were all dressed exactly alike, with their stiltlike muscular legs sheathed in pale pink tights under blue denim shorts. All three wore matching navy hooded sweatshirts, and each of them had her long hair fastened in a tight bun at the back of her head. They carried identical black bags as they walked quickly in short, measured steps, with their toes pointed slightly outward. Not one of them could have weighed more than ninety pounds.

Sami laughed quietly to herself. She could hear her grandmother's voice ringing in her head. "You could snap them like a wishbone," she would say. Sami's grandmother liked kids who ate—in her book, sharing an apple definitely wouldn't have qualified as breakfast.

"Darn baby bunheads," the alien-abducted woman moaned to Sami as she watched them toss the mostly uneaten apple into the trash. "I could have eaten that."

When the woman walked over to the trash can and began to fish around for the apple or any other discarded food, Sami took advantage of her temporary distraction to hustle her way out of the bus terminal.

As she opened the door and walked outside into the warm July morning, Sami gasped. Like Dorothy leaving her windblown cottage and entering Oz, she was overcome with the magical, colorful land she'd just entered. It was as though at that very moment she'd gone from a black-and-white existence to a brilliant Technicolor world full of sights, sounds, and smells that were beyond anything she'd ever imagined.

Well, Sami, she thought. *You're not in Kansas anymore.*

Actually, she wasn't in Elk Lake, Minnesota, anymore, but the sentiment was pretty much the same.

New York City. Sami smiled brightly at three young African-American teens playing Caribbean tunes on huge yellow, red, and orange steel drums. The teens were dressed in bright yellow short-sleeved shirts. Their hair was tied in tight dreadlocks. One of them grinned with hope at Sami and tipped his head in the direction of a small jar on the ground. Sami reached into her pocket, pulled out two quarters, and dutifully dropped them into the jar.

A few feet away from the drummers was a middle-aged Korean woman standing beside a large cart on which she'd stacked pieces of silver jewelry—small crosses, Stars of David, and five-sided pentagrams, all dangling from shimmering silver chains above rings that were shaped like skeletons and snakes. The woman sat quietly beside her stand, eating what looked to be some sort of dumplings. From time to time she would glance up, making sure that none of the passersby had made off with any of her jewelry.

Sami turned her head toward the other side of Forty-second Street. Standing only a few feet away were two women carrying briefcases. One wore a simple black dress. The other wore a black silk summer suit. Each had elegant white pearls around her neck. The women had sneakers on their feet so they could walk to their offices, but it was obvious from the shoe-shaped bulges in their briefcases that they had dress shoes in tow. The women checked their watches frantically and then hurried out into the street. As they headed down Forty-second Street, these corporate types didn't even seem to notice the drummers, the woman beside her silver stand, or the girl with big blue eyes who was watching them so intently.

She wriggled her shoulder slightly under the weight of her pale blue suede fringed pocketbook. She put down her suitcase for a second, taking care to place it between her legs. She squeezed her calves together and held the suitcase tight—her father had been certain to warn her that there were thieves everywhere in New York City. She wouldn't take her eyes off her suitcase for a moment.

Sami reached into her pocketbook and pulled out the *Guide to New York* that her brother Al had given her along with some cash to get her started. During the long bus ride to New York (actually, it had been two buses over twenty-nine hours), Sami had mapped out a plan of action. If she was going to get work as a fashion designer, she was going to have to get down to business as quickly as possible.

But first she would have to find a place to stay. Most of the hotel rooms listed in the *Guide to New York* were awfully expensive—$175 to $200 a night! But Sami had found a few that were cheaper. One, the Beresford Arms, cost far less—$65 for a small room. The guidebook described it as "a small haven for those on a budget, not far from the neon lights of Times Square." Sami thought it sounded perfect. After all, she was on a budget, and being just one person, a small room would be fine. And the name, the Beresford Arms, sounded very romantic, like a sophisticated New York version of an Italian *pensione*. Best of all, it was located at Forty-seventh Street and Tenth Avenue. Considering the Port Authority Bus Terminal was at Forty-second Street and Eighth Avenue, it couldn't be far. She checked the map in her guidebook and walked over.

The Beresford Arms might have been a nice hotel at one time, but as Sami walked into the lobby, all her dreams of old New York sophistication went out the door. The hotel was just plain old, with peeling red paint on the walls, and worn, musty, stained furniture atop worn, imitation Persian area rugs. It smelled strange, like a combination of body odor and mothballs.

But according to the sign above the counter, it was still $65 a night—quite possibly the cheapest in town.

"Can I help you?" a wrinkled, balding man with leering eyes asked Sami. He smiled slightly as he looked her over from head to toe, his eyes stopping for a moment to study her chest.

"I, um, I need a room," Sami said, nervously curling a lock of her long, thick, hair around her finger.

"For how long?" he asked her.

"I don't know," Sami said. "It depends. I'm not sure. . . ."

"I mean, do you need it for a few hours, or the whole night?" the man asked.

"A few hours?" Sami asked him, confused.

"Well, some of the girls around here . . ." The man studied Sami's makeup-free face, her burgundy and cream peasant blouse, and comfortably worn jeans. This was obviously not the attire his usual guests wore to work. "Nah, you're not one of 'em," he said finally.

"One of who?" Sami asked.

"One of the *working* girls," he told her. "We get a bunch of them. But you . . ."

Sami blushed. Somehow she knew that the term "working girls" wasn't referring to the women with the briefcases she'd seen walking out of Port Authority. "Oh, no!" she gasped, her face turning red. "I just need a place to stay until I find a job designing . . ."

The man laughed. "Relax, kiddo. It's okay. I got a nice room fer ya. Quiet, and private. And the bed's just been changed. All nice and clean." He turned around and grabbed a key from the wall of small cubby-hole mailboxes behind him. "Room 217, just up the stairs and to the right," he said. "I usually ask for the cash in advance, but you seem like a nice kid. I can trust ya. Just sign here." He pointed to a line in a ledger book.

She took the pen from the desk and nervously signed her name on the red line. "Thank you, um, Mr.——"

"Just call me Bud," he told her. "And if you need anything at all, just ask."

Sami hurried up the stairs and turned quickly toward the right. 211, 213, 215 . . . she breathed a sigh of relief as she placed the key into the door of room 217. Quickly she stepped inside and closed the door behind her, taking care to lock it tightly before she even dared breathe.

"Oh, my!" the blue-eyed beauty exclaimed as she flipped on the light and took her first look at her new home. The guidebook had said the rooms were small, but that didn't even begin to describe it. There was barely a foot of space between the door and the bed. And the only dresser in the room butted up against the foot of the bed, so that if she wanted to, Sami could literally unpack while sitting cross-legged on the threadbare floral bedspread that covered the lumpy mattress.

"I told you to get out!" a woman's voice rang out across the alleyway.

"I will not!" a man's gruff voice responded. "I'm the one payin' for this dive, y'know!"

Oh, brother. Bud had said the room was quiet. Obviously his definition of the word was different from hers. She climbed over the bed and closed the window. Within seconds, the smell of stale cigarettes and rancid air conditioning took over the room.

Sami thought about unpacking her bag, but finally decided against it. With any luck at all she'd have a job before the week was out—a job that paid her enough money to find a decent place to live. Not unpacking her bag was her act of defiance—of showing that she had faith in herself.

She'd be out of here before she knew it.

Still, for now, the Beresford Arms was home. And despite its less than luxurious appearance, it was a home in New York City. The thought filled Sami with excitement— and more than a twinge of homesickness. This was the first time since she left Elk Lake that Sami had been without a stranger in a seat next to her to talk to. The loneliness was suddenly overwhelming.

Quickly, she pulled out her prepaid cell phone and dialed a familiar number.

"Hello," a teenage girl's voice answered.

"Celia. It's me, Sami!"

"Sam! You made it! So, have you taken over the fashion industry yet?"

Sami laughed. "Celia, I've only been here an hour."

"That's fifty-five minutes longer than I thought it would take you," Celia teased.

Sami laughed. "Thanks for giving me five minutes."

"Well, you always were a slow starter."

The girls giggled together, just as they'd done for the past fifteen years.

"So, is New York everything you thought it would be?" Celia asked.

Sami looked around at the small, stifling room. "Well . . . it's different from Elk Lake, that's for sure."

"I'll bet," Celia agreed. "There are probably more people on your block than there are in our whole town."

"Probably," Sami agreed. Then she asked quietly, "So, how's my dad? Is he over my leaving yet?"

"Oh, you know Mac, he'll get used to the idea," Celia quickly assured her.

"I doubt it," Sami replied. "You should've heard him the night before I left. He was going on and on about how everyone abandons him. I mean, he's all alone now."

"I wouldn't say he was alone," Celia argued. "Al and I live a block away. Your aunt Rose lives across the street. And your grandmother is only in the next town."

"But I just keep picturing him sitting all alone in the living room, feeling abandoned by the women he loved."

Celia sighed. "It wasn't your fault she left."

"I know," Sami said slowly, remembering what it had felt like that cold

December morning when she was just ten years old. She'd come downstairs to breakfast only to find the note her mother had left for her, explaining why she'd had to leave. They'd never heard from her again. "But it's been hard for him all these years."

"I know," Celia agreed. "But you can't let that hold you back from what you want. I mean, is this your life or his?"

"That's not the point, Celia."

"It's exactly the point, Sam," Celia differed. "Your dad's happy in Elk Lake. Hell, he's only been to Minneapolis three times in his whole life, and that's just seventy-five miles away. Mac's an Elk Lake man—he likes being a big fish in a small pond. But you . . . Sami, you were suffocating in this place."

Sami thought about that. It was true. For as long as she could remember, she'd felt as though Elk Lake were closing in on her. She couldn't stand how everyone who came into her father's coffee shop seemed to know her business. Especially after Celia had become pregnant with Sami's brother's baby. Tongues were sure wagging after that. It seemed like all anyone could talk about was how Celia was a girl in trouble, and that Al had better make an "honest woman" out of her.

Which, of course, he had. A week ago, Al and Celia'd gotten married in a beautiful ceremony in the little church on the lake. Sami had designed the bridesmaids' dresses—pretty strapless black cocktail dresses that had caused a new Elk Lake scandal. No one in that tiny town had ever asked their bridesmaids to wear basic black and pearls before. In Elk Lake, black was for funerals—a thought that made Sami laugh, considering just how many women she'd already passed on the five blocks between Port Authority and the hotel who were wearing black outfits to their offices. Despite the warm July weather, black seemed to be the color of choice for New York women.

"So, where are you going to interview first?" Celia asked.

"I was thinking of going over to the Bridal Building in about an hour," Sami told her. "You know, that place we saw in the magazine that's just floors and floors of wedding designer showrooms. I have the sketches from your dress and the bridemaids' dresses. Then there are the designs I came up with for our prom dresses—I thought those could work as bridesmaid designs."

"The prom seems so long ago now," Celia mused. "Everything's changed."

Sami knew what she meant. Their senior prom had only taken place two months ago, but now everything was different. Celia and Al were married, and Sami was a thousand miles . . . *a whole world* . . . away.

"Do they have a maternity wedding gown showroom?" Celia joked.

Sami laughed, remembering how she'd had to change her design for Celia's dress when, all of a sudden, at the end of her third month of pregnancy, Celia had suddenly begun to show. "Wouldn't surprise me," Sami said. "This is New York, after all. So how's my brother?" she asked, changing the subject.

"Oh, you know Al," Celia said. "He'll never change. He's watching me like a hawk and making me crazy. Every five minutes it's, 'Did you drink enough milk? Have you had your protein today? Dried apricots have a lot of folic acid.' He's making me crazy. But what can I say? I love the jerk."

Sami giggled. "If you think it's bad now, just wait till the baby's born."

"I know, I know." Celia chuckled. "Look, Sami, I gotta run—I've got my monthly checkup at Dr. Gladstone's in twenty minutes, and if I'm a minute late, Al's going to have the whole police force out looking for me. Besides, you shouldn't waste a second more talking to me. You've got some pavement to hit. Now grab that portfolio I gave you, get out there, and put Elk Lake on the map!"

Sami smiled. Putting Elk Lake on the map had been a joke between her and Celia ever since they'd been in third grade and discovered that Elk Lake was too small to show up on any map of Minnesota. Back then, the girls had vowed that when they grew up they were going to become so famous that everyone in the whole state— or even the whole country—would know where Elk Lake was. Celia was going to dance her way to stardom, and Sami was going to design all her costumes. But with

Celia married and about to be a mom, it now fell to Sami to fulfill their childhood promise.

"It's as good as there," Sami promised Celia as she hung up the phone.

TWO

Midtown Manhattan in July was not a pleasant place to be. It was the height of the day, and the noon sun beat down from above onto Sami's head. More heat came up from the sidewalk and was trapped by the skyscrapers that stood tall on either side of the street. Cab drivers with their windows open to save money on air-conditioning screamed at messengers sweating their way through the streets on bicycles, and throngs of people pushed past one another on their way to their air-conditioned offices.

But Sami tried not to be affected by the heat as she walked along Broadway, clutching her black leather portfolio tightly under her arm. She was too focused on the task at hand to even think about the temperature. She studied the large numbers on the glass doors that lined Broadway. 1379, 1381, 1383, 1385. Ah, here she was. 1385 Broadway. The famous Bridal Building. It was one-stop shopping for any bride: gowns, bridesmaids' dresses, veils, flowers. Celia and Sami had read all about it in the bridal magazines they'd pored over in the weeks before Celia and Al's wedding. At the time, it had seemed like a fantasy world. Now, as she stood in front of the door, the fantasy was about to come true.

Sami walked into the lobby with a determined look on her face. She tried to appear as though she fit in with the other workers strolling in and out of the lobby. With any luck, she would be one of them soon. She quickly scanned the directory posted on the wall and spotted a familiar name—Très Joli Bridal Fashions. Celia had loved the Très Joli dresses in the magazines. They were simpler than most: white gowns with minimal lace and beading, classic cuts with a slight twist, making each one a little different from the one before it. Sami had based her design for Celia's gown on some of the Très Joli dresses, so it was only natural that she head up there first. She quickly stepped into the elevator and pushed the number 8.

The ride up to the eighth floor seemed interminable. She shared the elevator with two maintenance men who smelled as though they hadn't bathed in at least a week. Sami moved cautiously over to the other side of the elevator, taking care not to step on the toes of a woman in a tight black pantsuit and stiletto heels, and making sure she didn't bump into the two overweight men in shirtsleeves who were arguing over whether the Yankees should consider trading one of their starting pitchers.

With each opening and closing of the elevator doors, Sami's heart pounded a little harder. She was certain that if the ride took much longer, she'd have a heart attack, right here in the small, cramped elevator of the Bridal Building.

Luckily, she made it. Sami got out of the elevator and scanned the glass-enclosed showrooms: Francine's Flowers. Dream Wedding Veils. Samantha's Gowns. Très Joli Bridal Fashions—this was it. Without giving herself a chance to back out, Sami opened the glass door and walked inside.

The reception area at Très Joli Bridal Fashions was quiet. There was no one sitting on the black leather chairs that lined the walls, each positioned beside a stack of Très Joli bridal catalogs.

"Do you have an appointment?" a middle-aged African-American woman in a pale green suit asked sweetly as she walked out into the reception area.

"No, I—"

"We don't show the gowns without an appointment during the week," the woman interrupted. "Come back on Saturday. You don't need an appointment then."

"Oh, I'm not here to look at gowns," Sami assured her.

"Then why are you here?"

Sami lifted the heavy black leather portfolio onto the reception desk. "Actually, I'm a designer." She gasped a little, hearing the words come out of her mouth. It was the first time she'd ever identified herself as a professional. It sounded strange, but also impressive—and not at all false.

"Oh honey, you're in the wrong place," the woman said kindly.

"But I think if you'd just take a look at my designs, you'd see that I have that Très Joli feel," Sami pleaded.

"I'm sure you do. The thing is, our gowns aren't designed here."

"But this is the Très Joli showroom, right?" Sami asked.

The woman nodded. "Exactly. We *show* our gowns here. But we don't design or make them here. Our home office is in Paris."

Sami blushed. "Oh, I had no idea. I mean, the address in the magazine was 1385 Broadway and—"

"You're not from around here, are you?" the woman asked kindly.

Sami shook her head. "I'm from Elk Lake, Minnesota."

"Minnesota, huh," the woman mused. "You do sound a little bit like that wrestler who became a politician. You know, oh what's his name . . ."

"You mean Jesse Ventura."

"Yeah, that's him."

Sami laughed. Right now, former governor Jesse Ventura was pretty much the only person from Minnesota anyone outside of the state had ever heard of . . . but she was determined to change that. *Someday people will associate Minnesota with Sami Granger instead!*

"What's your name?"

"Sami Granger."

The woman held out her hand. "Ella Carmichael. Pleased to meet you, Sami." Ella stepped out from behind the counter and walked toward the black leather chairs. Sami followed and sat down beside her. "Do any of the bridal companies have designers here?" Sami asked anxiously.

Ella shook her head. "Not in this building, hon. I'm sorry. It's all showrooms. We mostly sell to retail stores. On Saturdays we open up to the public. That's when the brides come pouring in, looking for bargains. But the dresses aren't designed or made here."

Sami blushed harder and closed her portfolio. "Oh, I should have researched this better. I'm so embarrassed."

"Don't be embarrassed," Ella replied. "Most kids your age wouldn't have been brave enough to come to New York on their own, never mind march into a showroom with their designs in hand. You've got guts, that's for sure. Unfortunately, you don't have the know-how. Now I . . ." Before Ella could finish her sentence, the phone on the desk rang.

Ella jumped up and hurried over to look at the number that flashed across the screen on her phone. "Excuse me, it's my boss," Ella said as she picked up the receiver. "Hello, Mr. Loehr. Yes. I have it right here. Of course I can bring it to you right now. I'm just finishing up with something.

"I'm sorry," Ella apologized as she grabbed a folder from her drawer and hurried off to a room down the hall. "I hope you find what you're looking for."

"I think I may already have," Sami murmured as Ella left the room. She waited for a moment, making sure the older woman didn't return. Then she ran behind the desk and looked at the old-fashioned Rolodex that was sitting there.

Quickly, Sami looked at the list of names printed on the Rolodex cards. Ella was certainly well connected in the design business. Most of the numbers and addresses in her Rolodex were for bridal companies, but there were some other types of design houses as well: Mollie Mack, Ralph Lauren, Tara Davis Designs, Stella McCartney, Phat Fashions, Ted Fromme Fashions. It was an eclectic mix, to say the least. Quickly, she pulled a pen and paper from her bag and scribbled down as many addresses of design houses as she could find in the Rolodex.

Sami felt a little guilty as she speedily copied the numbers onto her paper. It was almost like she was stealing from Ella. Okay, not stealing exactly, but at the very least she was being extremely sneaky and underhanded. She could just hear her father now. "That's not the way I raised you, Samantha Granger," he would say.

But this wasn't Elk Lake, Sami reminded herself, in a desperate attempt to justify her actions. This was New York. And the only way she was ever going to get ahead was if she could point herself in the right direction. What was it Ella had said? Oh, yeah:

"You've got the guts. Unfortunately, you don't have the know-how." Well, Sami had now found out everything she needed to know.

Suddenly she heard footsteps from the room down the hall. Ella was coming back. Quickly, Sami hurried toward the elevator. Silently she made a promise to herself that she would thank Ella someday.

Someday when she was famous.

There was little sense in Sami hitting the pavement in search of a job that day. As she left the Bridal Building with Ella's address list in hand, the strain of traveling for four days straight was starting to get to her. Best to get a good rest and start out fresh in the morning.

By the time Sami returned to the Beresford Arms, the neighborhood was teeming with tourists out for pretheater dinners a few blocks away on "Restaurant Row." They seemed happy and excited to be in the Big Apple for their vacation— just the way Sami had felt when she'd gotten off of the bus a few hours earlier. Sami sighed. *Has it only been a few hours?* It felt like years since she'd arrived at Port Authority.

She walked through the dingy lobby of the Beresford Arms and over toward the stairway. But the path to the stairs was blocked by a couple making out on the first-floor landing. As they kissed, the man was breathing heavily. The girl, on the other hand, had a decidedly bored look on her face.

"Hey, take it upstairs, Chelsea," Bud shouted from the lobby. "Ya rented the room, now use it."

Chelsea sighed, took the man by the hand, and started up the stairs. "C'mon, you heard Bud. We gotta go somewhere more private."

Sami gave Chelsea and her "date" a head start before she climbed the staircase to the second floor. She didn't feel like running into them again. After she was certain they'd moved on, she hurried up to her room and closed the door behind her.

She undressed quickly and spent as little time as possible taking a shower. The water came out rusty, and the tub was old and stained. To make matters worse, Sami couldn't help but think about what had gone on in that shower over the years.

Getting out of the shower, Sami slipped into her favorite nightshirt—her father's old button-down striped shirt. It was nice and roomy, and very comfortable. Sami had never been able to figure out why women would want to sleep in itchy lace when they could just grab a man's shirt to sleep in.

Her stomach growled slightly. It had been hours since she'd eaten anything. That's when she remembered that Celia had packed her a tin full of cookies and other sweet treats for the trip. They made a delicious, if not exactly nutritious, dinner. But Sami was far too tired to go out and get anything else. She sprawled out on the bed and was soon asleep.

Three

Tara Davis Designs seemed as good a place as any to start her job search. Sami had always admired the company's simple, all-American look. In fact, she'd patterned some of her own sleeveless tees and soft wraparound skirts on their simple designs. There was plenty in her portfolio that would fit in with their stylish yet comfortable Rose Petal clothing line.

Unfortunately, Tara Davis Design's corporate offices were all the way uptown in the Seventies. It was a long walk from the Beresford Arms. She decided to take the subway just like any other New Yorker. Just the sound of being called a New

Yorker was magical to Sami. Besides, if she was going to make her life and her career in this city, there was no time like the present to start traveling underground.

The subway was everything Sami had heard . . . and less. The stench was almost unbearable in the heat—a mixture of urine and sweat. And the station was filthy. Someone had drawn a mustache and beard on a movie poster featuring Julia Roberts's smiling face. A photo of Shea Stadium had been defaced by another graffiti artist, who'd written the less-than-original slogan "The Mets Suck!" in big black letters. Sami clutched her portfolio tightly and stood close to the wall—taking care not to let her body actually touch the filthy white bricks. Despite the fact that it was already ten o'clock, way past rush hour, the train platform was still crowded. Sami made sure to stay away from the edge, for fear of falling onto the tracks.

When the train finally came, Sami hurried to find a seat. She squeezed in between a sweaty, heavy-set man in a pair of shorts and a white tank undershirt and a teenager in a black leather halter, jean shorts, and combat boots.

Just then, two men in matching black T-shirts entered the car. They stood near the door. "Welcome to the Underground Nightclub," one of the men said loudly. "For our first number, we'd like to sing 'When the Saints Come Marching In.'" The men then broke into a surprisingly good a cappella version of the song. As they sang, they walked through the train car, waving a jar of change under the noses of the passengers.

Sami sighed. This was definitely nothing like Elk Lake.

But then, that was the point, wasn't it?

Finally, the train reached the Sixty-eighth Street stop. As she walked up the stairs, she felt something warm and wet hit her head. She looked up at the gray sky. A sudden rain shower had begun. And not a clean, fresh rain like the kind back home. This was a hard, angry rain that was rapidly turning the dirty city streets into a muddy soup.

"Umbrella, umbrella!" a street vendor cried out.

Quickly, Sami rushed to his side. She pulled out three one-dollar bills. "I'll take one," she said.

"That'll be five bucks, lady," the vendor told her.

"But your sign says three dollars," Sami argued, pointing to a weather-worn cardboard sign glued to the man's cart.

"That was before it started raining," the vendor replied. "It's a matter of supply and demand. Now ya want one or what?"

Sami sighed and pulled two more dollars from her purse. The street vendor handed her a small black umbrella with a plastic handle. "Thanks, lady. Stay dry now," he said.

Sami put up her umbrella and walked up to Seventy-sixth Street. When she reached the address for Tara Davis Designs, she took a deep breath and headed for the elevator.

There was no mistaking the Tara Davis offices. As the elevator doors opened, Sami was greeted by the company's red rose logo on the wall behind a reception desk. Sami walked up to the receptionist and smiled. "I'd like to talk to someone about becoming a designer here," she said confidently.

"Do you have an appointment with one of our directors?"

Sami shook her head. "But I could make one. When will one of your directors be free?"

The receptionist sighed. "Just leave your résumé and some sketches."

"I'd much rather meet with someone personally," Sami insisted.

"Well, if they like your work, I'm sure you'll get a call."

"Are you certain someone will look at my work if I leave it?" Sami asked nervously.

"I'll forward it to the right department," the receptionist assured her in a tired, almost condescending tone.

Sami did as she was told, pulling out some copies of samples of designs she'd done that seemed in keeping with the soft yet fun Tara Davis designs. But somehow she had a feeling those sketches weren't going anywhere but on the bottom of a big pile.

As Sami walked back out onto Madison Avenue, she felt tired and overwhelmed. The rain had stopped, leaving behind thick, wet air that was hard to walk through. Sami could feel her long black hair going limp under the weight of the humidity. Her feet hurt, and her stomach was grumbling. She decided to take a break and have a snack. There was a deli on the corner.

"What can I getcha?" a young man in a white apron asked her as she entered the deli and walked up to the counter.

"Tuna salad on white bread with lettuce, and a cola," Sami replied.

"Soda's over there," the man said, pointing to a refrigerator with two glass doors. "Get your soda and pick up your sandwich at the cash register."

Sami went over and grabbed a can of cola and then walked up to the register. The cashier threw her sandwich and soda in a green plastic bag. "Eight sixty-nine," she said.

Sami shook her head. "There must be some mistake. I ordered a tuna sandwich and a soda."

"No mistake," the cashier said. "Eight dollars and sixty-nine cents."

"For a *sandwich*?" Sami asked incredulously.

"The tuna's seven bucks, the soda's a buck, and then there's the tax," the cashier replied, not bothering to hide the annoyance in her voice.

Sami sighed as she gave up the cash. She'd better find a job . . . and fast. She took the sandwich over to one of the small tables in the back of the deli and sat down. She unwrapped her seven-dollar tuna sandwich and began to eat hungrily. Then she gulped her soda and quickly headed toward the Ralph Lauren Polo offices just a few blocks away.

Unfortunately, the receptionist at Ralph Lauren Polo wasn't any more helpful than the woman at Tara Davis Designs. But Sami refused to give up. She simply climbed back onto the subway and headed to the corporate headquarters of Betsey Johnson. But while a woman from personnel had at least ventured out of her hot pink office to talk to her, she hadn't offered much hope, although she *had* taken a copy of Sami's designs and a résumé.

Back to the subway. This time she took the R train to Prince Street in SoHo. Climbing out of the subway, Sami felt as though she were in a completely different city. Gone were the tall skyscrapers and people with briefcases hurrying through crowded streets. SoHo was decidedly more relaxed than Midtown. The streets were narrower and were dotted with small café-style restaurants and art galleries. Less famous artists who were unable to get space in the galleries simply displayed their paintings and sculptures on the street, beside the rows of jewelry and sunglass vendors.

The residents of SoHo seemed less uptight than the people Sami had seen uptown. Their style of dress was far more funky—although black was still the color of choice. Instead of suits and dresses, the SoHo crowd seemed to like jeans and half shirts—with the obligatory pierced belly button proudly displayed.

This was the perfect atmosphere for the ultrahip Mollie Mack Fashions's headquarters. Sami felt hopelessly unchic and small town as she entered the huge loft space where the Mollie Mack designers toiled away each day. Next to the photos of Mollie's wild electric yellow, green, pink, and black lacy outfits that decorated the walls, Sami's simple pale pink terry cloth drawstring skirt and cream-colored cap-sleeved top seemed awfully out of place. And the funky electronic music that was piped into the waiting room was like nothing Sami had ever heard before. Back home she was more likely to run into music by the Dixie Chicks or Faith Hill than Beck.

Still, Sami was sure she could learn to fit in with the mod fashions that Mollie and her designers created. All she needed was a chance. And if anyone could understand that, it would be Mollie Mack.

It was unbelievably exciting for Sami to be in the Mollie Mack headquarters. Mollie was legendary in the fashion world. Sami knew her life story by heart. She'd started out as a kid from a poor neighborhood just outside of Boca Raton, Florida, back in the 1950s. She always said that her love of bright colors came from being raised near the beach. Mollie hadn't stayed in Boca Raton very long. As soon as she was old enough to get a passport, she flew off to London and became part of the mod scene on Carnaby Street during the swinging sixties. She'd designed outfits for everyone from Twiggy and Edie Sedgwick to Mick Jagger and David Bowie. But while many of Mollie's sixties and seventies contemporaries had long since worn out their welcome in the fashion industry, Mollie, like her friend and rival Betsey Johnson, had stayed current. Today her fashions were as hot as ever. She had boutiques in New York, Los Angeles, London, Tokyo, Paris, and Milan, and high-end department stores like Saks Fifth Avenue and Lord & Taylor also sold her fashions.

Mollie's small-town background had always made her a hero to Sami. She knew that if she and Mollie could meet somehow, there would be an instant connection. All she had to do was get her foot in the door.

"I'd like to speak to someone about a design job," Sami said as she walked up to the reception desk.

"What school are you with?" asked the receptionist, a tall, thin blonde in a neon green miniskirt and a black lace blouse.

"I'm not with any school. I'm a designer," Sami replied.

The receptionist eyed her carefully. "You look like you're in school."

Sami shook her head. "No, I'm a designer."

"Any experience?"

Sami nodded. "I've done some theater work, costuming," she replied ambiguously. There was no point in adding that the theater was in the Elk Lake Regional High School, and that her design work had been limited to the costumes for her senior class production of *Bye Bye Birdie*. "And I've designed custom gowns for weddings." *One wedding, actually, but that fact was also best kept secret.*

The receptionist smiled at her. "Well, we usually give internships to kids from FIT or RISD, but . . ."

"FIT? RISD?" Sami said.

"Fashion Institute of Technology and Rhode Island School of Design. Sometimes we get kids from Cooper Union, or NYU, but mostly . . . ," the receptionist began. She handed Sami an application and shrugged. "Fill out the information. Maybe you'll get lucky. The interns get really wonderful experience."

"Interns?" Sami said. "You mean like doctors?"

The receptionist giggled. "Not exactly. The interns work here for a semester to get experience. It looks great on your résumé to say you worked at Mollie Mack. Mollie makes it a point to let the kids get real designing experience, not just photocopying and answering phones."

"Wow!" Sami exclaimed. "I think that's exactly what I'm looking for."

"Mollie pays her interns too," the receptionist boasted, as though being paid for work was some sort of innovative concept.

"How much does the job pay?" Sami asked her.

The receptionist pointed to a figure on the application. Sami gasped. It was less money than she'd earned working at her father's coffee shop after school.

"It's not huge, I know," the receptionist admitted. "But it's better than most. Some internships don't pay at all, but Mollie thinks it motivates the interns to work harder. And we do give credit toward graduation. Of course, since you're not in school . . ."

Sami looked at her strangely. "But everything in New York is so expensive and . . ."

The receptionist looked at her kindly. "Well, we have a sales job available at our Columbus Avenue store. That pays better. And you get a ten percent discount on Mollie's clothes. Maybe you'd be interested in applying for that?"

Sami sighed. "I'll think about it," she said as she quietly turned and headed back toward the elevator.

Stepping back out into the New York heat, Sami could feel her eyes welling up with tears. *What an idiot I am,* she thought ruefully. *What made me think I could just walk in and get a job? I'm nothing special. I'm just a nobody from Elk Lake, Minnesota.*

And maybe that's where I belong.

Sami crawled back into the dark, dismal hotel room she'd learned to call home. She sat down on the bed and pulled out her cell phone. She sighed as she punched in Al and Celia's phone number.

"Hello?"

Sami would know her brother's deep voice anywhere. Just the sound of it brought tears to her eyes. "Hi, Al," she said, her voice cracking slightly.

"Samster!" he greeted her. "How's my favorite New York celebrity?"

"It's lonely at the top," Sami told him. "It's also lonely at the bottom."

"No luck today, huh?" he asked her gently.

"None. But it's okay. I'm learning to get used to the sound of doors slamming in my face."

Al sighed. "Those design houses don't know what they're missin'," he assured her.

"All I want is a chance to show 'em," Sami said. "How's Celia?" she asked, changing the subject.

"We heard the heartbeat yesterday," Al said proudly. "Amazing."

Sami sighed. She'd only been gone a few days and already she'd missed something as incredible as the sound of her niece or nephew's heartbeat. If she were still in Elk Lake, she could have gone to that doctor's appointment and heard it too. "I wish I'd been there," she told Al sincerely.

"You can't be here. You have to be in New York making us proud," he replied, sounding as supportive as possible. "Look, my bride here is grabbing for the phone. So I'm gonna go. Hang in there, baby sis."

"I'll try," Sami replied. But she didn't sound particularly convincing.

"Hey, Sam!" Celia got on. "How's it going?"

"Lousy," Sami admitted. "I couldn't even get anyone to make an appointment to see my designs."

"Where'd you go?"

"The Bridal Building, which, by the way, doesn't have any design studios. Then I tried Tara Davis, Ralph Lauren, Betsey Johnson, Mollie Mack—"

"Well, you sure went straight to the top," Celia said.

"I only get rejected by the best," Sami joked bitterly.

"Maybe you have to start out smaller," Celia suggested. "Aren't there any lesser-known design houses you can try?"

"Well, there's one on this list of design houses I have—" Sami began.

"Oh, cool. How'd you get a list like that?" Celia interrupted.

"I, um, I got it from a woman at the Bridal Building," Sami said quickly. *It wasn't exactly a lie.*

"So what's the name of the company?" Celia asked her.

"Ted Fromme Fashions," Sami read from the list of names she'd gotten from Ella's Rolodex. "I think they do mostly sportswear."

"Well, you're a sporty kind of gal. You can design casual clothes."

"At this point I'd design *dog* clothes!" Sami told her.

"Well, let's try this Ted Fromme place before you head over to the House of Hound," Celia teased.

Sami giggled. "You never fail to cheer me up," she thanked her best friend.

"That's why I'm here," Celia vowed.

As soon as she hung up the phone, Sami pulled out her portfolio and flipped through the sketches, looking for something similar to the simple yet elegant sportswear she believed Ted Fromme Fashions was trying to making a name in. After pulling out a few pages of simple skirts and blouses, as well as a few

drawings of slacks and capri pants, Sami
laid her head on the small, musty pillow
and fell into a sound sleep.

It had been a long day.

Four

Sami's stomach grumbled as she stepped onto the elevator of the small office building on Thirty-eighth Street and Seventh Avenue, where Ted Fromme Fashions was located. Sami had hoped to save a few dollars by skipping breakfast, although in the back of her head she could hear her father's voice scolding her for the decision. "It's the most important meal of the day, Samantha," he'd say in his thick Minnesotan accent. "You're like a fine race car. You gotta put gas in the engine before you can hit the speedway."

Sami sighed. At the moment, some of her dad's huge blueberry pancakes would feel really good. But she couldn't think about that now. She had to focus on the task at hand: making a good impression at Ted Fromme Fashions. Of course, making sure that her stomach stopped grumbling would be a good start in that direction. Sami quickly reached into her bag and pulled out a lint-covered mint Life Saver. *Breakfast of champions,* she thought ruefully as she popped the mint into her mouth.

The elevator door opened on the eleventh floor. As Sami stepped out into the hallway, she heard an angry man's voice bellowing from one of the offices. "Just answer the phone! It's been ringing off the hook for the past fifteen minutes!" he shouted furiously.

"I'm taking my break now!" a woman shouted back. "*You* answer it."

"Now is not a good time for you to take your break," the man replied, sounding angrier now.

"I'm entitled to a smoke break and I'm taking it," the woman told him.

"Fine, take it in twenty minutes, or even ten minutes. Just not now," the man barked at her.

"Sorry, but my nic fit won't wait another second," the woman replied.

"If you walk out that door, don't bother coming back in!" the man threatened.

"Sounds good to me," the woman answered. "Have a nice life, Bruce!" She opened the door and darted out into the hallway, flying past Sami on her way to the elevator.

"Um, excuse me, do you know where Ted Fromme Fashions is located?" Sami asked, reaching out a hand to stop the irate woman.

The woman frowned and pointed her unlit cigarette toward the door at the end of the hall. "I wouldn't go in there, if I were you," she warned Sami. "It's a total hell house! And Bruce Jamison is the devil himself!"

The vehement tone in the woman's voice frightened Sami, and for a moment she considered following the woman into the elevator and straight out of the building. But Sami knew she had to go in there. Ted Fromme Fashions was at the bottom of her list. There were very few chances left. She had no choice but to give this one her best shot.

The reception area of Ted Fromme Fashions bore little resemblance to the reception areas at Tara Davis, Ralph Lauren, Betsey Johnson, and Mollie Mack. Those were sophisticated businesses, and when Sami entered each room, she could feel a sense of professional excitement all around her.

By contrast, the Ted Fromme reception area was sheer *chaos*! Instead of catalogs neatly piled on small end tables, there were sheets of paper all over the couch and table. Rather than being painted a sophisticated white like at Tara Davis Designs, or Mollie Mack's shocking pink, the walls at Ted Fromme Fashions were a dingy tan, more fitting for an accounting firm than a design house. And instead of funky music being piped in through speakers in the wall, the only music here was the sound of phones ringing off the hook. And instead of an organized receptionist at the front desk, the only other person in the room was a stressed-out young man in a half-buttoned shirt with rolled-up shirtsleeves, who stood staring at the phones with a look of sheer panic on his face.

But seeing that the panic-stricken man behind the desk was the only one there, Sami walked up to the desk. "Excuse me?" she started.

"What do you want . . . ?" he bellowed angrily. Then he raised his eyes and stared at Sami. He seemed to be disarmed for an instant. "I'm sorry," he apologized. "It's just that these phones won't stop, and Roxie, our receptionist, just quit and . . ."

Sami was well aware that Roxie hadn't exactly quit—it was more like she'd been given an ultimatum and had taken this man up on his threat—but she kept her mouth shut.

"Anyway, what can I do for you?" the harried man asked with a half smile that suddenly struck Sami as rather sexy.

"Well, I'm actually looking for someone in personnel," Sami began. "You see, I'm interested in applying for a job."

The man's half smile now stretched fully across his face. "Are you an angel?" he asked her suddenly.

"Excuse me?"

"Well, I think you must have been sent from heaven."

Sami's big blue eyes registered her confusion.

The man behind the desk laughed. "You're looking for a job, right?" he asked her.

Sami nodded.

"And it just so happens I'm in the market for a new employee. Can you answer a phone?"

"Well, sure, but I'm not . . ."

He pulled out a chair from behind the reception desk. "Then the job's yours," he told her. "Start with line six. Just take a message."

"I was actually . . ." Sami was about to tell him that she was looking for a job in the design department, not the reception area. But the truth was, any job would be good right around now. She only had enough money in her wallet for two more nights at the Beresford Arms, and that was only if she didn't eat. Sami needed cash. And this was a foot in the door—even if she hadn't gotten past the reception desk.

Sami slipped into the seat and picked up the phone, pressing down the button for line 6. "Ted Fromme Fashions," she said in her most professional voice. "How may I help you?"

The man in the button-down shirt waited until Sami had taken messages from the three callers Roxie had left on hold. Then, when things had settled down a bit, he dragged a chair over beside Sami. "Hi there," he said, putting out his hand. "I'm Bruce Jamison. And you are . . ."

"Sami Granger."

"Welcome to Ted Fromme," Bruce said with a bright smile. "You couldn't have come at a better time."

"What do you do here?" Sami asked, suddenly wondering who this man was and whether he had any authority at all to hire her.

"I'm a junior designer," Bruce told her in a voice filled with pride. "I'm also the office manager. In a place like this, everyone's got two jobs . . . at least."

Sami smiled. "Well, you're getting varied experience."

Bruce laughed. "That's what we need around here. A little optimism. And"—he stopped for a moment and studied Sami's body and face—"and a lot of beauty. You know, when you first came in here, I thought you were one of the models for the fall show."

Sami blushed. "I'll bet you say that to all the girls."

Bruce shook his head. "That's one bet you'd lose." Just then, the phone rang again. "You'd better get that," he said. "But I'll tell you what. I'll take you to lunch at twelve. We can talk about your salary, responsibilities, and all that other dreary stuff then."

Yes! Sami practically jumped up and down, but at the last second she remembered she needed to make a good impression and instead she nodded and picked up the phone. "Ted Fromme Fashions. How may I help you?"

"That's just what I like to see. A girl who likes to eat," Bruce teased as he watched Sami twirl a huge portion of spaghetti onto her fork and put it hungrily into her mouth.

Sami chewed for a moment, swallowed, and smiled. "I guess I'm kind of hungry," she confessed. "I didn't eat breakfast. And I didn't expect to start working today."

"It was kind of quick, wasn't it?" Bruce admitted. "But that's how things work at Ted Fromme. Think about it. When I started with Ted, I was right out of college. That was two years ago. No one had heard of us. Now we've got a show coming up in New York, and possibly another one in Milan. You're in on the ground floor of a great company, Sami." He took his napkin, reached across the table, and gently wiped a dribble of tomato sauce from her chin.

That act, so innocent and yet so intimate, sent a shiver through Sami's body. All through lunch she'd had a tough time not being obvious about just how handsome she thought Bruce was. His big green eyes were the first thing you noticed about him, but there was plenty more eye candy to go around. His mouth had an easy smile that lit up his oval-shaped face. And underneath that button-down shirt lay a pair of broad shoulders and some pretty substantial muscles. And the way he ran his fingers through his thick, neatly cropped sandy blond hair was enough to cause several female heads to turn his way.

But if Bruce noticed the women in the restaurant drooling over him, he didn't show it. Instead, his focus was completely on Sami. "Okay, so now I bet you're wondering what you'll be making, and what kind of insurance we have, and when you can take your first vacation," Bruce said, suddenly sounding quite businesslike.

Actually, Sami hadn't been thinking about any of that. She'd just been so excited to have a job and to be eating in this incredible New York restaurant. Still, she didn't want to seem completely naive. "Yes, I have to admit that's all very important to me," she said, trying to sound as sophisticated as she could.

"Well, we can't start you at a big salary, but our last receptionist was making thirty-five, and I suppose you should earn the same."

"Thirty-five thousand dollars?" Sami asked.

"Is it too low?" Bruce asked her nervously. "Because I really can't go any higher."

Sami had no idea whether that was a low salary for New York. It sounded like an awful lot of money to her. She didn't know any other eighteen-year-old who was earning that much.

"Oh, and we have full medical coverage for all our employees. You get two weeks' vacation, but you can't take any of it for four months."

Four months. Quickly, Sami did some calculating in her head. Celia was three months pregnant now. She was due in January. That was a good six months away. All right. She'd be able to get home to meet her new niece or nephew.

Bruce laughed at the bright smile that suddenly flashed across her face. "I see you're already thinking about that vacation," he mused, his voice regaining the more playful tone he'd had before. "So, are you seeing anyone?" he asked her casually as he deftly returned the conversation to a more personal nature.

"No," Sami admitted shyly. "I sort of outgrew the guys I went to school with. They all thought I was crazy to want to come here. Girls in my hometown don't usually want careers."

"But you do?" Bruce asked, staring into

her eyes so intently that it made her blush.

"Oh, yes!" Sami exclaimed. "I want to be a designer. It's the only thing I've ever wanted. Even when I was little, when the other girls were playing wedding, I was drawing their dresses and then making them out of old sheets."

"Sort of shabby chic wedding gowns," Bruce joked.

Sami giggled. "Something like that. Anyway, I knew I wasn't going to get anywhere staying in Elk Lake."

"Elk Lake." Bruce smiled broadly and chuckled at the sound of it.

"What's so funny about that?" Sami asked, suddenly defensive.

"It's just that it sounds so . . . small-town Americana. I sort of imagine a town with one Main Street that has a butcher shop, a barber shop, a coffee shop, and a sheriff's office."

Now it was Sami's turn to laugh. "That's it exactly."

"New York must be quite a shock," Bruce ventured a guess.

"Not as much as I thought it would be," Sami admitted. "I think there's a part of me that's always belonged here more than in Elk Lake. But then again, there's a part of me that will always be Elk Lake."

"You can take the girl out of the country but you can't take the country out of the girl."

Sami grinned. "That's what they say."

"Well, I think you're going to fit in here," Bruce assured her. "Especially at Ted Fromme's. It's a small company, but that means you get a close-up look at every aspect. I've sat in on design meetings, accounting meetings, advertising meetings, and promotion retreats. You're not going to get that opportunity at the big houses."

"Do you think Ted would look at some of my designs?" Sami asked excitedly.

Bruce didn't answer. Instead, he glanced down at his watch. "Whoa. We've got to get back to the office. Those phones are probably ringing off the hook!"

Sami's first day at work went quickly. Within a few hours she'd met several of the employees and could recognize them by face, if not by name. When the phones weren't ringing, she neatened up the reception area, placing Ted Fromme catalogs near the couch, the way she'd seen in some of the other houses. She suggested to Bruce that they bring in a stereo, or at the very least a boom box, to play some mood music, and he'd agreed to see if they could requisition the necessary money from petty cash.

She was so busy that she was literally shocked when Bruce came out from the back office and told her to go home. "What are you still doing here?" he asked her.

"I just wanted to finish inputting everyone's phone extensions into my computer," Sami replied.

Bruce seemed impressed. "I knew Roxie was lazy, but I had no idea how little she was actually doing. In one day you've done more than she managed in the whole three months she was here."

"Thanks," Sami said proudly.

"But you don't have to get it all done in one day," he continued. "A gorgeous girl like you should be at home getting all dolled up to go out clubbing or something."

Sami frowned. "I'm not much of a clubbing person," she admitted.

"Don't knock it till you've tried it," Bruce urged her.

"I don't know where any of the clubs are. And I wouldn't go alone, anyway."

Bruce nodded slowly. "Well, I've got to spend tonight working on some designs to show Ted, but I could show you around sometime."

Sami felt a twinge of jealousy. Bruce was designing clothes while she was putting together a personnel directory. Still, at least she had a job. And he *was* awfully nice. "I'd like that," she said honestly.

"Now go home," Bruce urged.

"I just need to—"

"Hey, I'm your boss," Bruce interrupted. "And I say go home and relax."

Sami piled into the subway car with the rest of the rush hour crowd. She held her portfolio tightly under one arm and held on to the overhead handrail with her other hand. As the car moved along its underground track, Sami felt a rush of excitement. These people were all New Yorkers heading home from work . . . and she was one of them!

When the train stopped at Forty-second Street and Eighth Avenue, Sami got out and headed over to the Beresford Arms. She was exhausted. The thought of taking a shower—albeit a lukewarm, rust-tinged shower—beckoned her. For the first time she couldn't wait to get to the little room on the second floor of the hotel.

But when she reached the Beresford Arms, there were police cars blocking the street. Several men and women in blue uniforms were standing on the side-walk, exchanging notes with two detectives in black slacks, white shirts, and silver badges. Sami tried to walk past them and into the hotel, but one of the officers stopped her.

"I'm sorry, miss, but you can't go in there," he told her.

"Why not?"

The police officer was obviously not used to having his orders questioned. "It's a police matter," he said simply.

"But this is where I'm *staying*," Sami continued.

"Well, hopefully you can get back in there in an hour or two."

"But—"

"Look, kid," the officer said firmly, "we're investigating a murder here. No one's getting in that building until our forensics team has had a chance to get all the evidence they'll need. If I let everyone traipse in and out, we'll have a bunch of contaminated evidence."

"A murder!" Sami gasped. "But who? How?"

"I can't tell you that," the officer replied in an official tone. "We're not releasing any information to the public at this time. But I can tell you one thing: This isn't the first murder I've seen in this joint. The clientele here aren't exactly strangers to crime. What's a nice kid like you doing here, anyway?"

Sami could feel tears welling up in her eyes. "I'm not exactly sure," she murmured.

"Well, I'd find another place to stay if I were you," the officer said as he turned and walked back toward a group of his fellow police.

Sami began to cry as she watched the officer walk away. She'd never experienced anything like this before. The worst crime she could remember happening in Elk Lake was the time some high school kids knocked over a bunch of mailboxes on Halloween. *Murder* . . . If her father heard anything about this, he'd come and drag her home.

Still, at the moment, Sami had no place else to stay. She'd have to wait until the police could let her back in, and then first thing in the morning she'd look for a new home. For now, there was nothing else to do but take a long walk.

As Sami walked along Tenth Avenue, she struggled to regain her footing. But no matter how hard she tried to focus on something—anything—other than the murder, her mind kept racing back to what the policeman had said. "The clientele here aren't exactly strangers to crime." It was a scary thought.

The longer she walked in the heat, the more tired and frightened Sami became. The sound of a truck backfiring almost sent her running for cover. So she was happy when she found a nice quiet place to stop in and rest her feet. The Fresh Brew Coffeehouse was a coffee shop just like her dad's place in Elk Lake. But other than serving coffee, the two establishments had nothing in common. At her dad's place, people sat at the counter or in booths, sharing their experiences over coffee and a slice of pie or a sandwich. But here, there were no welcoming booths. Just small round tables with one or two wooden chairs beside them. There were only five customers in the coffee shop, and no one was talking to anyone, although one woman was having an animated conversation on her cell phone.

Sami ordinarily would never have any caffeine this late in the day, but who knew how many hours it would be before she'd be allowed back into the Beresford Arms for the night?

"An iced coffee, please," Sami told the girl at the counter.

"Sure. Do you want an iced latte, skim latte, soy latte, iced cappuccino, iced mochaccino, or iced espresso?"

"Just iced coffee," Sami repeated.

"You're sure?"

Sami nodded.

"Oh, that's a problem," the girl murmured.

"Why?" Sami asked her.

"I've never made one of those."

Sami sighed. "Never mind. I'll just have an iced tea."

"Raspberry, green, citrus, or black tea?" the girl behind the counter asked.

Sami sighed. Who would have thought ordering iced tea could be this complicated? "Black tea," she said finally.

"Do you want whole milk, skim milk, soy milk, or lemon with that?"

"Just black iced tea in a glass with a straw," Sami said in a measured tone.

"You don't have to get nasty," the girl barked back.

Sami sighed, instantly shamed. "I'm sorry. I just found out that there was a murder in the hotel I am staying in and—"

"Ooo! I heard about that. You're at the Beresford Arms? That place is *gross*."

Sami nodded. "I know. But it was all I could afford when I got here. Now I'm going to look for an apartment, although

I'm not even sure where to start. I can't spend a whole lot on rent."

"Did you check the bulletin board?"

"What bulletin board?"

The girl pointed to a board on the far wall of the coffeehouse. "Sometimes people post ads for roommates there. Maybe you can find something. Most of the people who come in here are artists and musicians, so they need someone to split the rent." She handed Sami her iced tea. "Here you go, one plain black iced tea."

"Thanks," Sami said. "How much?"

"Two-fifty."

Sami sighed. *Two dollars and fifty cents for an iced tea! Amazing.* Still, if she could get a lead on an apartment, it would be worth the investment. She took the glass of tea and walked over toward the bulletin board. There were plenty of signs posted. GUITAR LESSONS FROM A PRO . . . ARE YOU LOOKING TO LOSE WEIGHT, FAST? . . . PROFESSIONAL DOG WALKER LOOKING FOR WORK! . . . DAILY DANCE CLASSES . . . *ROOMMATE* WANTED.

Sami's eyes focused on the ad for a roommate. In smaller print, it read:

Female nonsmoker seeks same to share East Village one-bedroom walk-up. No pets allowed. $450 a month. Contact Rain G.

The ad gave the phone number and address of the apartment. Sami wasn't wasting any time. She pulled out her cell phone and quickly dialed the number on the paper.

"Hello," a woman answered.

"Hello," Sami replied. "I'm looking for Rain G.?"

"This is Rain."

"Oh, hi. My name's Sami. I'm calling about your advertisement. Are you still looking for a roommate?"

"Yes," Rain replied. "When would you like to come over and see the apartment?"

"Would now be too soon?" Sami replied anxiously.

Five

"Did you have any trouble finding the place?" Rain G. asked Sami as she opened the door and gave Sami her first view of the apartment.

"Not too bad," Sami said, looking around. "Your directions were perfect. I would have been here sooner, but the train stopped in between stations for a while."

"Let me guess," Rain joked. "The conductor told you the problem was a fzzpz-zfzzpzz."

Sami giggled. The tall, redheaded woman had done a perfect imitation of the garbled announcement that came over the subway loudspeaker.

"So come on in," Rain said. She led Sami into the apartment. "I'll give you the grand tour." She held out her arms and pointed at the worn couch, two black chairs, card table, stereo, and TV. "This is the living room, dining room, and TV room. Over there's the kitchen, such as it is. It's pretty small, but I don't mind because I eat a lot of take-out. The bathroom's over there." She pointed to a closed door. "And the bedroom is right through here."

Sami followed Rain into the bedroom. It was small, although not as small as her room at the Beresford Arms. Rain had divided the single bedroom in two with the use of a screen decorated with Asian women collecting water.

"And that's it," Rain said, walking back into the living room. "Not much of a place, but it's home."

"It looks amazing compared with where I've been staying," Sami assured her. "The Beresford Arms is awful. There was a murder there today!"

"Yeah, that's not the greatest place," Rain admitted.

"You know it?" Sami asked.

"No," Rain replied. "But I've heard of it. And I know places like it. I stayed in a few of them when I first got here."

"You're not from New York?" Sami asked.

Rain laughed. "No. I'm from Carmel Gardens, Virginia. It's a really small town. If you're ever driving through, don't blink. You might miss it."

"Sounds like my hometown."

"Where's that?"

"Elk Lake, Minnesota."

Rain nodded understandingly. "And let me guess, everyone there thinks you're nuts for moving here."

"Well, not everyone," Sami admitted. "My brother and sister-in-law think it's great. But the rest of the people in town . . ."

"I know; I've been through it." She waved her hand a bit. "So has just about everyone else I've ever met here."

"Really?" Sami said.

"Sure. Sometimes I don't think there really is such a thing as a native Manhattanite."

Sami looked at Rain. It was hard to believe this thin, sophisticated young woman had ever lived in a small town. She looked totally downtown New York in her black jeans and green Juicy cropped tee. Her ears were pierced several times—she had at least four hoops in each one. And she'd no trace of an accent. "How long have you lived in New York?" Sami asked her.

"'Bout a year," Rain replied.

Sami hid her amazement. Was it possible that in one short year she might look as downtown hip as Rain did?

"So what do you do?" Rain asked, settling down in one of the chairs and indicating Sami should sit.

"Well, I want to be a designer," Sami told her. "I mean, I *am* a designer. But right now I'm working as a receptionist at Ted Fromme Fashions."

"Ooo, Ted Fromme. They make some nice stuff. Do you get a discount?"

"I don't know," Sami admitted. "I could ask."

"That would be cool."

"So, what do you do?" Sami asked.

"I'm a model."

"Wow!"

"Oh, it's not all that impressive," Rain admitted. "Everyone in this neighborhood is either a model, an actress, an artist, or a musician. We're all also waiting tables."

Sami giggled.

"But just because I serve veggie burgers at Dojo doesn't mean I'm not a real model," Rain continued, folding her long legs beneath her on the couch. Her large hazel eyes grew animated as she talked about her fledgling modeling career. "I'm with an agency and everything. Chic Modeling. Have you heard of them?" Sami shook her head. "Well, they're pretty big. And they think I have a lot of potential. So far all I've done are a few catalog shots, but I'm hoping to get some runway work during the Bryant Park shows this year."

"That would be really exciting," Sami agreed, having no idea who Bryant Park was or what he designed.

Rain was about to answer when suddenly the bathroom door opened and a guy walked out. He looked to be about twenty-four or twenty-five years old. He was tall and dark haired, and had eyes the color of coffee with just a drop of cream in them. But his most noticeable features were his broad shoulders and a killer set of six-pack abs—a fact Sami noticed right away, since he wasn't wearing anything more than a pair of cut-off shorts and a pair of sneakers.

"Oh hey, Vin," Rain said as he came into the living room. "I'd almost forgotten you were here. This is Sami."

Sami gulped. Rain must have a boy-friend. She wondered if he stayed in the apartment often. There was only that thin Japanese screen between the beds, and Sami didn't think she'd be comfortable with Rain and this Vin person right next to her doing, well, whatever they might be doing.

Rain was looking at Sami and laugh-ing. "I know what you're thinking," she told Sami. "And don't worry. Vin doesn't stay here. He lives across the hall. He was just fixing a leak in the shower. If I had to wait for the super to do it . . ."

"I was glad to help." Vin turned his amaz-ing eyes toward Sami. "Self-preservation . . . The thought of Miss Workout Queen over here not being able to shower was just too gross for me. The smell of pierogi coming from the Russian restaurant down the block is bad enough!"

Rain tossed a couch pillow at Vin. "Thanks, buddy. Just what I needed, you telling a potential roommate that I stink."

"I didn't say you stink . . . just that we'd all be in trouble if I didn't fix that shower."

Rain turned to Sami. "Watch out for this guy," she warned. "He grew up in Brooklyn. You know no one from the OBs can be completely trusted."

Sami tore her gaze from Vin and looked at Rain curiously. "OBs?"

"Outer boroughs," Vin explained. "Brooklyn, the Bronx, Queens, and Staten Island. Rayna here is a total Manhattan snob."

"Can I help it if I don't see any point in hanging out with the bridge-and-tunnel crowd?" she teased back.

"Rayna? Oh, I'm sorry," Sami apologized quickly. "I thought you said your name was Rain."

"It is," Rain assured her.

"Oh, right," Vin teased. "That's your name *now*. But all your friends and family at home call you Rayna. It's Rayna Goldfein," he told Sami.

"Oh, no!" Rain exclaimed suddenly. "You've told her my deep, dark secret. I'm sorry, Sami, but now I'm going to have to kill you."

For a moment, Sami stared at her, not quite sure if she was kidding.

"Relax, kiddo, it was a joke," Rain pointed out.

Sami smiled nervously. "I knew that. I'm just a little shaky after what happened at the Beresford Arms."

"There was a murder at the hotel where she's been staying," Rain explained to Vin.

"That's tough stuff to deal with," Vin consoled her. "Anyone you know?"

Sami shook her head. "No. I don't know anyone there. I kind of keep to myself." Talking about the Beresford Arms made Sami nervous. She quickly changed the subject. "What made you change your name?"

Raina shrugged. "The agency decided that Rayna Goldfein didn't have enough pizzazz. So now I'm just Rain G."

"I like it," Sami assured her.

"I like *you*," Rain replied. She held out her hand toward Sami. "This is going to work out great. Two small-town girls in the big, bad city. We could take over!"

Sami reached out and shook Rain's hand, sealing the deal.

"Heaven help us," Vin teased.

"You'd better watch out," Rain teased back. "Now it's two against one in this hallway. Country girls versus Brooklyn boy. You don't stand a chance."

Vin looked back into Sami's blue eyes. "I think I'm lost already."

It was almost eleven o'clock before Sami had a chance to check in with Celia and Al. Luckily, with the time difference, her best friend and her brother were still wide awake.

"Hello?" Celia answered.

"Hey, Celia!" Sami replied excitedly. "Guess where I am?"

"The Plaza Hotel?" Celia asked.

"No."

"The Staten Island Ferry?"

"At this time of night?" Sami said, surprised.

"You're right," Celia agreed with a laugh in her voice. "Where could you be calling from at eleven at night, New York time? How about prison?" Celia teased.

Sami giggled. "Of course not."

"Okay, I give up. Where are you?"

"In my *apartment*!" Sami squealed.

"You got an apartment already?"

"Yup, *and* I got a job!"

Now it was Celia's turn to squeal. "You got a design job? Ohmigod! This is so exciting!"

"Well, it's not that exciting," Sami admitted. "It's not exactly a design job. But I *am* working at a design house. I'm the receptionist at Ted Fromme Fashions."

"Oh." Celia clearly struggled not to sound disappointed. "Well, at least you're in the door. Maybe you can get someone there to look at your designs."

"That's what I was thinking. My boss is a junior designer, so he'll look at them." Sami thought for a moment. Bruce hadn't exactly said that he would look at her portfolio—but he hadn't said he wouldn't, either.

"What's your boss like?" Celia asked.

"Nice," Sami assured her. "He's very supportive. He took me out to lunch today. We have a good time at the office. And he's got the biggest green eyes, and a great smile."

"Sounds like Sami's got a crush . . . ," Celia teased.

"No." Sami denied it vehemently— maybe *too* vehemently. "I'm just describing him, that's all."

"Okay." Celia didn't sound convinced.

"Ceil . . ."

It was Celia's turn to giggle. "So tell me about the apartment. Where are you?"

"In the East Village, just off St. Marks Place. I have a great roommate. Her name is Rain, and she's a model."

"Wow! A model! How cool is that?" Celia seemed suitably impressed.

"It's a lot of fun around here," Sami assured her. "Everyone's so nice. The guy across the hall's a carpenter from Brooklyn. He's nice, but he's really tough. You wouldn't want to mess with him. He went up to the hotel with me to get my stuff, and he convinced the manager not to charge me for today, since I wasn't sleeping there or anything." Sami smiled, remembering how Vin had stood tall over Bud, threatening him without even saying a word. Bud had crumbled like a pile of dust. "And by the time we got back here, Rain had brought in pierogis for dinner."

"What are pierogis?" Celia asked.

"Oh, they're these Russian potato-onion crepe things. They're so delicious. I've never eaten anything like them!"

"Everything sounds really great, Sami," Celia said with a voice slightly tinged with envy.

Sami knew Celia well enough to sense the small drop of melancholy in her tone. There was a time Celia had had big dreams too. But now, with the baby and all . . . Immediately, Sami changed the subject. "So, what's new with you?"

"Well, I think I might have felt the baby kick," Celia whispered into the phone.

"How cool is that!" Sami exploded. "Al must have flipped."

"Al doesn't know," Celia whispered.

"Why not? And why are you whispering?"

"Because I'm not sure it was really the baby kicking. It felt like a little flutter, but it could have been gas. Anyway, I don't want Al getting all excited until I'm sure. You know how he gets. He'll have his hand on my stomach all the time, and you can't even feel it from the outside yet."

"Oh Celia, I wish I were there with you for all this," Sami said honestly.

"Just make sure that cute boss of yours gives you time off at the end of January to come home and meet your little niece or nephew."

"Oh, I'll be there," Sami promised. "I wouldn't miss it for *anything*."

"I know," Celia replied softly. "But you'd better hang up and get some rest. You're a working girl now!"

"Gee, I am, aren't I?" Sami said excitedly. "Hey, will you tell my dad I'm okay?"

"You haven't called him yet?" Celia asked her.

"I've tried to, a few times. But I always hang up before he can answer. It was so bad between us before I left. I'm sort of afraid to talk to him."

Celia was quiet for a minute. Sami

knew her best friend—and now sister-in-law—was remembering how Mac Granger could get when he was crossed. She also knew that he was still extremely angry at Sami for leaving Elk Lake. Everyone in town knew it. Even before she left, Mac wasn't shy about sharing his frustration with Sami with just about everyone who walked into his coffee shop. No, Sami wasn't wrong for not calling her dad just yet.

"Don't worry, Sam, he'll come around," Celia said finally. "And when he does, I'll make sure he calls you."

"Thanks."

After giving her best friend her new phone number and address, Sami hung up the phone and walked into the darkened bedroom. She could hear Rain snoring softly from her bed on the other side of the screen. Moving quietly so as not to wake her roommate, Sami set her alarm for 6:30 and climbed into her very own bed in her very own apartment.

Six

When the downstairs bell rang Saturday evening, Sami's heart skipped a beat. "That's Bruce," she called out to Rain from the bedroom. "Could you buzz him up? I'm not ready yet!" Sami's tone was filled with excitement that had been building for quite a while. She'd been working at Ted Fromme for almost three weeks now, and this was the first time Bruce had made good on his promise to take her out and introduce her to the New York club scene.

"You're kidding," Rain called back. "You've been getting ready for this date since this morning."

"It's not a date," Sami reminded her as

she walked out into the living room. "Bruce just volunteered to show me a little bit of the New York nightlife."

"Uh-huh," Rain replied, sounding completely unconvinced. "I know *I* always spend an hour on my hair and makeup when I'm just hanging out with a friend." She pressed the button by the buzzer to let the front door of the building open, then she opened their door to the hallway a bit. "He's on his way," she warned Sami as soon as she heard the sound of footsteps coming up the stairs.

"Oh, no! Do I look okay?" Sami asked nervously.

Rain laughed. "Why? Does it matter? I mean this isn't a *date* or anything, is it?"

Sami rolled her eyes, stuck her tongue out playfully in Rain's direction, and then ran back into the bedroom for one last check in the mirror.

"Oh, very mature," Rain teased. She looked out into the hallway, where Bruce was making his way to the apartment. "You must be Bruce," she greeted him.

Bruce smiled as he approached the door. "That's me," he replied. "And you must be Rain."

"The one and only. Come on in. Sami's almost ready."

Bruce walked into the apartment and looked around. "I used to live in a place like this when I first moved to the city."

"Really?" Rain said. "But you don't anymore?"

Bruce smiled. "I've moved on. Now I'm in an elevator building on Eighty-second and Riverside, just off the park. Good thing, too, since I'm on the fourteenth floor."

Rain nodded with recognition but didn't say anything. She knew the neighborhood Bruce had mentioned—small, overpriced apartments in prewar buildings. People paid for the address, not the accommodations. "I'd offer you a snack, but the refrigerator's kind of empty," Rain told him. "I've been teaching Sami the fine art of take-out."

"That's okay," Bruce replied. "I grabbed something on my way here."

"So where are you guys going?" Rain asked, flopping down on the couch and folding her legs into a long pretzel.

"I thought we'd hit Promise for a while.

Sami's never been to a club in the city, and I figured that's a good place to start."

"It's certainly one of the big names in New York nightlife," Rain replied. "Me, I like the smaller places. You know, neighborhood bars, local clubs."

"Well, to each his own," Bruce replied, a bit dismissively for Rain's taste. He looked at his watch. "I wonder what's taking her so long?"

"I just had a few more finishing touches," Sami told him as she made her entrance from the bedroom.

Bruce jumped up from the couch. "Whoa, look at you!" he exclaimed.

Sami looked down at her black dress. "Do you like it?" she asked shyly.

"Oh, yeah," Bruce assured her. "Is it one of your own designs?"

Sami nodded. Actually, it was one of the bridesmaids' dresses from Celia and Al's wedding. Sami had spent the morning turning it into something appropriate for a New York dance club by trimming the skirt so it had an asymmetrical hem. She'd had to sew the whole hem by hand since her sewing machine was still back in Elk

Lake, but from the look on Bruce's face, it had obviously been worth it.

"Well, come on, we need to show New York what a Sami Granger original looks like!" Bruce urged, taking Sami by the elbow.

Sami smiled.

"Don't wait up," Bruce told Rain. "I plan to have this magnificent creature out dancing all night."

"Oh, I'll be up," Rain assured him. "I'm just like a vampire. You know, asleep all day and awake all night."

Promise was crowded by the time Bruce and Sami arrived at the club. People were lined up three rows deep by the bar, and the dance floor was filled with sweaty couples moving to the beat of the music. Sami recognized a few of the songs—one by Shakira, another by Justin Timberlake, and one she was pretty sure was by Madonna. They were similar to songs she'd heard on Top 40 radio, except they'd been remixed to include a dance beat.

"You want a drink?" Bruce asked her.

Sami shook her head. "I'm underage."

"No one here cares about that," Bruce told her confidently. "Come on, have something. It'll loosen you up."

"I really just want a Coke," Sami insisted. The truth was, she didn't want to loosen up too much. This was her first time in a real New York club. She wanted to be totally alert and take it all in.

"Coming right up," Bruce said. "Wait right here. And don't go dancing with anyone else while I'm up at the bar. Tonight you're all mine."

Sami watched him as he headed off for their drinks. He really was remarkably handsome, and he seemed so confident and comfortable in this environment. While Sami found the lights and the music disconcerting, Bruce seemed as relaxed here as he did in the office. Despite the crowd of people around the bar, Bruce somehow managed to maneuver his way right up to the front of the line. Within a few seconds he was joking with one of the bartenders while their drinks were being poured. Sami expected someone to argue that Bruce had butted in front of them, but no one complained. It was as though everyone around him just assumed Bruce was someone deserving of special treatment.

Which was saying a lot. Bruce wasn't the only good-looking guy in the club. Everyone there seemed to be beautiful and stylish. It was as if the bouncer outside the club would only let attractive people inside. Sami looked at herself in the mirror. Sami had never thought of herself as particularly beautiful, or particularly unattractive. She was just Sami. But tonight, among all these gorgeous New Yorkers, she felt suddenly awkward, as though this were some sort of club that she never could have gotten into on her own without someone like Bruce as her sponsor. It wasn't a very good feeling. She hoped that one day she'd feel as though she really fit in, the way Rain and Bruce so obviously did.

"Here you go, one Coke," Bruce said as he returned to Sami and handed her the drink. He held out his martini glass. "To us," he toasted.

Sami clinked her glass against his. "To us," she agreed.

"Let's dance," Bruce suggested.

Ordinarily, Sami would have begged

off. She wasn't big on dancing in public. That had always been Celia's thing. At their school dances, Celia had boogied the night away while Sami had stood off to the side, chatting with friends and making mental notes on how she might change the design of the dresses other people were wearing. But tonight, Sami wanted to dance. She didn't know if it was the excitement of being out with Bruce, or just the overall vibe in the club, but Sami was happy to place what was left of her Coke on a nearby table and follow Bruce onto the dance floor.

Bruce was an excellent dancer. He rocked smoothly to the beat, his arms and legs moving just enough to be cool without being too affected. As they danced together, Bruce moved close to Sami until she could feel his warm breath on her neck. Feeling him so close made Sami want to shiver. She had to fight the urge to wrap her arms around his neck and pull his body against hers.

"Whew, I'm getting hot," Bruce said after he and Sami had been dancing for quite a while. "You want to take a break, get some air?"

Sami shrugged. "Sure, if you do."

"What, you're not tired?"

"Nope. This is all too exciting."

Bruce wrapped a strong arm around Sami's waist. She tensed slightly and then relaxed against his elbow. "We've been here for over two hours," he told her.

Sami looked surprised. "Really? It didn't seem that long at all."

"Time flies when you're having fun," Bruce murmured lazily in her ear. Sami had to fight to keep her knees from buckling as she followed Bruce from the club.

"I'd better take you home," Bruce said as they reached the street. He put out his arm and waited for a taxi to come to a stop in front of them. Then he opened the car door and let Sami hop in.

"First Avenue and St. Marks," Bruce told the driver in his sure, confident tone. Then he leaned back on the seat and wrapped his arm around Sami's shoulders. "Did you have fun?" he asked her.

"The best time in my whole life," she replied honestly. "I've never been anywhere like that before."

"I've never been out with anyone like

you before," Bruce replied. Then he leaned over and kissed her on the lips.

At first Sami thought to remind Bruce that the taxi driver could see them through his rearview mirror. But the power of Bruce's kiss knocked any rational thoughts from her brain. She found herself slipping quickly under Bruce's spell, and she kissed him back with a passion that matched his own. Her back was pressed against the car door, but she could barely feel the handle jabbing into her back. Her mind was elsewhere; all she could think about was the warmth of Bruce's body leaning against her own, and the soft wetness of his lips as his tongue struggled to meet hers.

"Um, 'scuse me, pal," the cab driver said as the car came to a sudden stop. "But do you want the near or far corner of St. Marks?"

The sound of the driver's voice shocked both Sami and Bruce back to reality.

"This is fine," Bruce mumbled as he sat up abruptly.

Sami opened the door of the cab and stumbled out. Her legs felt all weak and jellylike as she stood on the pavement.

Bruce paid the driver and got out onto the sidewalk beside her. "Oh, you don't have to—" Sami began.

"Door-to-door service," Bruce assured her. "Besides, I'm not ready to say good-bye to you just yet."

Sami smiled at him as she fumbled around in her handbag for her keys. Then she opened the door and she and Bruce began the long climb up the stairs to the apartment.

Sami could hear music coming from her apartment before she reached her door. There were also the sounds of people laughing, and a strange smell she didn't recognize leaking out into the hall.

"Sounds like your roommate's got a party going on," Bruce remarked.

"Well, it's Saturday night. I wonder who's here?" Sami replied as she unlocked the door and walked inside.

There certainly was a party atmosphere in the apartment. Rain was sitting on the floor surrounded on either side by tall, thin, blond boys. One had long straight hair; the other, a crew cut and a soul patch growing on his chin. All three of them were laughing and sipping on beers. Across the room, Vin was busy by the stereo, looking through the CDs with the help of a tall, willowy brunette who was obviously flirting with him. Vin, however, didn't seem to be noticing.

"Hey, look who's home—it's the design darlings!" Rain shouted across the room. She stood up and waved her arms. "Ladies and gentlemen, may I present the toast of the New York fashion world, Sami Granger and Bruce . . . Bruce . . . what did you say your last name was?"

"I didn't," Bruce replied. He turned to Sami. "I think your roommate is drunk," he noted, rolling his eyes slightly.

"Shows what you know," Rain told him. "I'm not drunk. I'm not high. I'm just in a great mood. We're celebrating."

"What are we celebrating?" Sami asked.

"I got a gig!"

"A what?" Sami asked.

"A gig. A *job*," Rain explained. "I'm going to be on the runway when Mollie Mack displays her new line in the fall!"

"Oh, Rain! That's awesome!" Sami raced over to hug her roommate.

"Mollie Mack, eh?" Bruce mused. "Is that old hag still designing?"

"Of course she is," Sami replied, not noticing the disparaging tone in Bruce's voice. "Mollie Mack is huge!"

"She's been around forever," Bruce commented.

"And she's still really hot!" Rain informed him.

"I guess," Bruce agreed. "I just meant that she's sort of yesterday's news."

"Oh, and you're today's news?" Rain asked.

"Well, Ted Fromme is, anyway," Bruce said. "And I design for him."

Sami began to sense the tension growing between her roommate and Bruce. "I think this is great, Rain," she congratulated her. "And maybe one day you can be in one of our shows too."

"You never know," Rain agreed, lifting a bottle of Diet Coke to her lips.

"So, did you have fun?" Vin asked as he made his way across the room and gave Sami a friendly peck on the cheek.

Immediately, Bruce moved closer to Sami and put his arm around her waist.

"We've been dancing the night away," he told Vin. Then he stuck out his free hand. "Bruce Jamison," he introduced himself. "And you are . . ."

"Vin DeSanto. I live across the hall from these two wild women."

"Vin's an unbelievable carpenter," Sami told Bruce. "A real artist."

"Is that so?" Bruce murmured. He seemed utterly uninterested.

The two men eyed each other, but neither said a word. Instead, Rain stood up and raised her soda bottle high. "To New York's fashion world!" she shouted. "Long may we reign!"

"Speaking of which," Bruce said, turning his attention back to Sami, "could you bring that portfolio of yours to work on Monday? If the designs in there are anything like this dress you're wearing tonight, I think Ted would be very interested in seeing them."

Sami threw her arms around Bruce's neck. "Oh, Bruce! I could just kiss you!" she exclaimed.

That was all the encouragement Bruce needed. He placed his lips on hers and kissed her long and hard, running his hand through her hair for extra effect. For a moment there was an uncomfortable silence in the room.

"Marking his territory," Sami heard Vin whisper to Rain.

"Like any other dog," Rain whispered back.

Seven

Sami was sitting in the living room sketching when Vin knocked on the door on Sunday morning. "Hey, wake up, you sleepyheads!" his deep voice called through the door.

Sami walked over and opened the door. "You're too late, Mr. Alarm Clock," she teased. "We've been up for hours."

Vin walked into the living room. He stopped for a moment, listening to the CD playing on the stereo. "Mmm . . . a Bach concerto," he remarked. "I gather Rain's not here."

Sami shook her head. "She went out for a run about an hour ago. Then she said something about a manicure and pedicure. She's got a big meeting over at Mollie Mack tomorrow. Sorry."

"Don't be sorry," Vin replied. "Who said I was here to see her? Besides, I love Bach."

"You do?" Sami sounded surprised.

"I was raised on classical music. Of course, in my house it was mostly Italian opera, but I'm a huge fan. It's nice to have company around here. Your roommate is more the headbanger type."

"I know. But that's kind of neat too. It's new to me. And there are actually some good melodies hiding in there from time to time."

"Good melodies in Kid Rock?" Vin asked. "I never thought about that." He flopped down beside Sami on the couch and looked at her sketches. "You work too hard," he remarked.

"Well, you heard Bruce. He wants to see my designs tomorrow. So I thought I'd work on a few new ones."

"Oh yeah, *Bruce*," Vin said slowly. "I wouldn't pin all my hopes on that one."

Sami looked at him curiously. "You don't like him?"

Vin shook his head. "I just don't trust him."

"You don't really know him," Sami declared.

"Not him, necessarily," Vin admitted. "But I know a lot of people like him. Big on flashin' cash and compliments."

Sami shook her head. "You're wrong. He's a really nice guy. And he's incredibly supportive of my work. I mean, he might actually show some of my stuff to Ted Fromme. That's a huge deal."

"Just watch out for him, okay?" Vin said quietly.

"Why? Do you have some sixth sense I don't know about?" Sami teased.

"Just street smarts, I guess." He seemed to study her for a moment. "Look, I have an idea," he said, changing the subject. "Since we both like classical music, why don't we go hear some? The Philharmonic is performing in Central Park later."

"I'd love to," Sami replied. "But I don't get paid until Friday, and I don't have any money to spend on tickets."

"Don't worry about that," Vin assured her. "The concert's free. It's out on the

Great Lawn. The acoustics stink, but it's a good program—Bernstein, Beethoven, and Mahler. And you'd have great company."

Sami smiled. "You're on."

"Great!" he exclaimed, his brown eyes lighting up with excitement. "I'll tell you what. I'll go get my picnic basket and a blanket to sit on. Then we'll head over to Balducci's, pick up a few sandwiches, some cannolis for dessert, and maybe a bottle of wine."

"Some what?"

"Cannolis. They're a kind of Italian pastry. My grandmother used to make the most incredible ones, but the kind they sell at the bakery are pretty good. You have to try the ones that are stuffed with vanilla cream and chocolate chips."

"Sounds good," Sami agreed. "But, how much—"

Vin shook his head. "This one's on me," he told her. "You can get the cannolis next time."

"Well, in that case, you've got a deal."

"You don't mind if we take the subway uptown, do you?" Vin asked her.

"No, why would I?"

Vin shrugged. "I don't know. I guess you must have taken a cab last night and . . ."

"Oh, that was different."

Vin frowned slightly. "Yeah, I guess it was. Anyway, I'll go change and get the picnic basket and I'll be back in a flash."

Sami began to giggle.

"What's so funny?" he asked.

"You are," Sami explained. "I never thought you'd be the type of guy to get so excited about classical music—or to own a picnic basket, for that matter."

"Oh, there are a lot of things you don't know about me, Sami," Vin assured her with a mysterious look. "I'm just full of surprises."

As Sami slipped into her black cotton capris and white terry tank top, she hummed a bit of Beethoven's Fifth to herself. There was none of the nervous excitement she'd felt the night before when she was getting ready for her date with Bruce. Instead, Sami felt calm and relaxed, the way she always did when Vin was around. He was her buddy. Someone to hang out with, laugh with, and listen to classical music with. True, he could be a little over-protective at times, but that just made Sami like him more. He was kind of like her brother Al that way, always wanting to take care of her. Vin was sort of like a combination friend and big brother. Maybe that was why she felt so comfortable around him.

By the time Vin returned to Sami's apartment with his picnic basket, he was a changed man. He'd showered and shaved, and somehow managed to comb his unruly, curly brown hair into something resembling a hairstyle. "Ready to go?" he asked Sami when she answered his knock on the door.

"Sure," Sami agreed.

"You don't need to check your hair, or grab a lip gloss or anything?"

Sami seemed confused. "Why would I want to do that?" she asked. "We're just going to the park. I don't need to get all made up, do I?"

Vin smiled. "No. I think you look great just the way you are. Do me a favor, Sami?"

"What?"

"Don't ever turn into a New York girl."

"What are you talking about?" she asked him.

"I don't know," Vin answered. "It's just that I think Elk Lake must be an incredible place."

Vin had been right about the sound system in Central Park. Despite the massive speakers set up throughout the Great Lawn, the acoustics in Central Park weren't the greatest. And it didn't help that the people didn't exactly behave like they were in a concert hall. Many of the audience members spent a lot of time talking on cell phones, giving directions to late-arriving friends. Sami wished she had a quarter for every time she heard someone say, "I'm right near the ball field. Can you see me? I'm waving at you." And as the evening went on and the bottles of wine emptied, many people in the audience grew giggly and restless. The few couples who'd made the brave attempt to bring babies to the concert found themselves scrambling to keep their offspring from crying.

Still, Sami wouldn't have traded the

evening for anything. It was so thrilling being in Central Park, together with hundreds of New Yorkers, as the New York Philharmonic played music on the huge stage at the edge of the Great Lawn.

Before she'd left for New York, Sami had heard all the horror stories about Central Park—her father had seen to that. He'd come home every night with some other urban myth he'd heard about the dangers that lurked in the park. Until this moment, Sami couldn't have imagined ever being in Central Park after sunset. Yet, sitting there on this evening, with Vin at her side, she didn't feel at all afraid. She knew he'd take care of her.

Just as he'd promised, Vin was full of surprises. He knew all kinds of interesting information about the composers of the music they were hearing, especially Leonard Bernstein. Bernstein was a sort of cultural hero in New York. Besides being a conductor of the Philharmonic Orchestra, he'd written several shows, including *West Side Story*.

When the concert ended, Vin and Sami joined the throngs of other New Yorkers heading out of the park and spilling onto the streets of the Upper West Side.

"Do you have to rush home?" Vin asked her.

Sami shook her head. "Not especially. Why?"

"I wanted to take you to my favorite coffee place," he replied. "I know you'll love it. And it isn't far from here at all."

"Sounds good," Sami agreed as she followed him down Central Park West and into a small restaurant on one of the side streets.

A chubby older woman with gray hair and just a slight mustache greeted them at the door. "Vincent!" she shouted, giving Vin a hug. "I haven't seen you in months."

"Mrs. Biondi," Vin replied, pecking the woman on the cheek. He stepped to the side and pulled Sami toward her. "I want you to meet my friend Sami. She just moved in across the hall."

"Hello, Sami," Mrs. Biondi greeted her. She turned back to Vin. "It's so nice to see you. You don't come here so often since your uncle Peter moved to Florida."

"I promise to come more often now. And I'll bring Sami."

"That's what I want to hear," Mrs. Biondi told him. "You two kids want a nice quiet table in the garden?"

"Sounds perfect," Vin replied.

Mrs. Biondi led Vin and Sami through the restaurant and out the back door. Sami was shocked as they entered the yard. It had been transformed from a small lot behind a restaurant into a secret garden, complete with grass, two trees, shimmering white garden furniture, and a beautiful stone fountain. "I'll bring you your favorite," Mrs. Biondi told Vin. She turned to Sami. "And what would you like?"

"What's your favorite?" Sami asked Vin.

"Iced cappuccino with chocolate sorbet in it. "

"Mmm . . . I'll have one too," Sami said. "But better make mine a decaf. I'll be up all night otherwise."

As they waited for Mrs. Biondi to return with their drinks, Sami looked around at the other people in the garden. It was a funny thing about New York. People dressed differently depending on the neighborhood. Like in SoHo, everyone wore black. On the

Upper East Side, it was designer sportswear. And here, on the Upper West Side, the women all seemed to wear jeans and light T-shirts with varying styles of mules for shoes—sort of a casual chic look that cost way more than one would expect.

"So how do you like New York?" Vin interrupted her thoughts.

"I love it," Sami replied honestly.

"But it must be different from Elk Lake."

Sami giggled. "That's for sure. I can't even imagine what my friends at home would think of the people in our building. In Elk Lake, blue hair is for old ladies—not for Mohawks. Some of Rain's friends . . . I mean, they're really nice. But all those tattoos and earrings that people have . . ."

"No one has earrings in Elk Lake?" Vin asked her.

"Well, the *girls* do—in their ears. And usually just one per ear. But guys with earrings? Or pierced tongues and noses? I saw someone with a pierced *eyebrow* the other day, and—"

"You'd be surprised what people pierce in our neighborhood," Vin teased.

Sami grimaced. "I guess I don't get it."

Just then Mrs. Biondi came by with two tall frappé glasses, each filled with cold cappuccino. A huge scoop of chocolate Italian ice sat precariously on top of the coffee. "I gave you each an extra scoop of chocolate," she said as she handed them straws and long-necked ice cream spoons. "Just like I used to do when you were a boy."

"Thank you so much!" Vin squealed, looking and sounding remarkably like a kid as he dove into his chocolate ice.

As the woman walked away, Sami grinned at Vin. "This place is amazing. You must come here a lot."

"Not as much as I used to. But it's always been one of my favorites. When I was a kid, my uncle would bring me here. He would tell me stories about how opera stars would come by for a late cup of tea after a performance at the Metropolitan Opera House. And how John Lennon and Yoko Ono would sit for hours at that table back there just gazing into each other's eyes." He pointed to a secluded table near the fountain.

"Oh, I wish I'd been there for that." Sami sighed. "John Lennon was my father's idol. I was raised on the Beatles."

"You like the Beatles?" Vin seemed surprised.

Sami nodded. "You know, someday their work will be considered classical music. I think it'll live on forever."

Vin grinned. "In that case, I have another surprise for you."

After they'd finished their iced cappuccino, Vin led Sami back toward the park. He stopped in front of a huge old building at the corner of Seventy-second Street and Central Park West. Sami was pretty sure she'd seen its pointed roof and gargoyles in a picture somewhere. As she stood in front of the giant gated courtyard in the center of the building, she had a sense of familiarity. And yet she couldn't quite place it.

"This is the Dakota," Vin explained. "They filmed *Rosemary's Baby* here."

Sami nodded. *Rosemary's Baby* was one of Al's favorite old horror movies. That's where she'd seen the building before.

"A lot of other celebrities have lived here too," Vin continued. "Leonard Bernstein died here. And Lauren Bacall and that sports announcer John Madden still live here. But I guess the biggest thing that ever happened was that John Lennon was shot right there." He pointed to the entranceway of the building, not far from the little booth where the Dakota security guard stood.

Sami looked at the ground, imagining John lying there bleeding to death while Yoko Ono frantically screamed for help. The thought was too much to bear. Tears suddenly began to stream from her eyes. It was impossible for her to control them, which was pretty embarrassing considering they weren't the only people standing outside the courtyard. Three tall, blond guys, all speaking German, had gathered there as well and were in the process of taking photos of one another standing in front of the building.

Much to Sami's relief, Vin didn't laugh at this sudden burst of emotion. He put his arm around her shoulder and held her close, wiping away a few tears of his own. "Gets me every time," he admitted as they stood there for a moment, just staring at the spot on the ground.

"Where have you two been?" Rain asked as Sami and Vin walked into the apartment at about eleven o'clock that night.

"Vin took me to hear the Philharmonic in Central Park," Sami explained. "It was *unbelievable*. You should have seen the fireworks after the concert. And then he took me to this little coffeehouse where John Lennon and Yoko used to hang out. So naturally we just had to go see the Dakota, and—"

"Wow, you certainly got the deluxe tour," Rain said.

"I aim to please." Vin laughed.

"And you succeeded," Rain continued. "Look at this girl! Sami's practically bursting!"

"Oh, and speaking of bursting, we had an amazing picnic with these incredible desserts," Sami continued, as if to prove Rain right. "They were pastry shells with cream and topped with powdered sugar. What did you call them?"

"Cannolis," Vin replied.

"Don't even mention dessert," Rain moaned. "Anything with sugar is off-limits until after this fashion show. Mollie Mack's clothing is totally unforgiving."

"Okay, well, the music was really interesting too," Sami assured her in an attempt to change the topic. "I hadn't heard much by Leonard Bernstein before, but he wrote this ballet score—"

Before Sami could finish her sentence, the phone began to ring. "You'd better get that. It's gonna be for you," Rain told her.

"Why do you say that?" Sami asked.

"Because he's been calling here all night, wondering where you are."

"Who?"

"Bruce Jamison," Rain replied. "Who else?

At the sound of Bruce's name, Sami's eyes lit up. She leaped across the room and dove for the phone. "Hello?" she said excitedly. "Oh, I'm sorry. It was all so spur of the moment. I went to Central Park with a friend to hear the Philharmonic," she continued as she took the portable phone into the bedroom and shut the door.

Rain studied Vin's face as he watched

Sami disappear into the other room. It wasn't hard to catch the look of disappointment in his eyes. "Uh-oh. I don't like the looks of this."

"What are you talking about?"

"She's just a naive, eighteen-year-old kid, Vin. Don't do it."

"Do what?"

"Fall for her," Rain replied simply.

"Too late," Vin admitted as he turned and walked out of the apartment.

Eight

Sami was the first one in the office on Monday morning. She'd brought her portfolio, just as Bruce had requested, and was anxious to show it to him as soon as he arrived. But Bruce was far from an early bird. Usually most of the employees arrived way before he did.

The day certainly started on a positive note. Ted Fromme arrived only minutes after Sami. The designer actually smiled, and called her by name.

"Good morning, Samantha," he greeted her with her given name. Sami usually hated her full name, but hearing Ted say it in his soft Southern drawl gave it a certain sense of artistic drama that she kind of liked.

"Good morning, Ted," she replied. Three weeks and she was only just starting not to act nervous around him.

"Is Bruce Jamison in yet?"

Sami shook her head. "But I expect him any minute," she promised Ted, anxious to keep Bruce out of any trouble.

"When he gets here, tell him I need those designs on my desk by Friday if he's going to have anything represented in the Fall Show," Ted said. There was a vague sense of urgency in his voice that showed he wasn't pleased that Bruce was waiting until the last moment to deliver his work.

"Oh, I think he was working on those all weekend," Sami lied.

Ted looked skeptical but didn't say anything disrespectful about Bruce. Instead, he complimented Sami. "That's some dress," he drawled. "I like the way the neck is cut."

"Thank you. I—"

But before Sami could tell Ted that the

scoop-necked tank dress was her own design, he turned and walked back toward the design offices.

It was more than a half hour before Bruce finally rolled into the office.

"Good morning," Sami greeted him enthusiastically.

"Morning," Bruce mumbled.

Sami looked at him, confused. His voice lacked any of the intimacy it had had on Saturday night, and his face gave no sign of his usually mesmerizing smile.

"Um, Ted said to tell you that he needs your designs by Friday," Sami told him.

"I don't need you rubbing it in," Bruce snapped at her.

"I'm just delivering the message," Sami said helplessly.

Bruce took a deep breath. "You're right." He mustered a slight smile. "Is that dress one of yours?" he asked her.

Sami nodded. "Ted told me he liked it," she told him proudly.

"Ted has good taste," Bruce agreed. "What did he say when you told him it was your design?"

"I didn't get a chance to tell him," Sami said. "He was so busy."

Bruce nodded. "Did you bring your portfolio?" he asked casually.

"Oh, yes!"

"Good." Bruce finally gave her his bright smile. "Let's meet tonight after work, in the conference room. We can call in for sandwiches and look at your stuff after everyone's gone home."

"That would be great," Sami replied excitedly. "I really appreciate your helping me like this, Bruce."

Bruce placed one strong hand on her arm. Sami could feel her whole body tingle.

"There's nothing I would rather do than help you," he assured her with a playful wink.

Sami was certain that the day was going to take forever after that. But the truth was, time actually flew. The phone was ringing off the hook, with calls from Milan and Paris, and even Hong Kong. Sami made a mental note to call Celia and tell her she'd spoken to designer and fabric manufacturers from all over the world. That was the kind of thing Celia would find exciting.

Then, some potential models for the Fall Show arrived for go-see meetings with Ted. The girls were all so similar, with their dark, shoulder-length straight hair and long, thin, fluid bodies, that Sami wasn't sure how Ted would be able to tell them apart. But it was obvious that Ted had a specific look in mind for his show, and he had put the call out to the modeling agencies to send over the girls who fit his description. Sami had offered the girls something to eat, but not one of them had taken her up on it. Instead, they'd all asked for water with lemon.

Sami was so busy that she was surprised when Bruce stopped by her desk around six o'clock. "Everyone's gone, babe," he told her. "Come on, let's go in the back."

Finally! Sami's stomach jumped at the thought of Bruce looking at her portfolio. He was a professional designer. His opinion meant a lot. Her fingers shook a little as she turned off her computer and programmed the telephone lines' automatic response message. Then she picked up her portfolio and followed him into the conference room. "Do you want me to call in for some sandwiches?" Sami asked him. "Are you hungry?"

Bruce smiled lasciviously. "Not for sandwiches," he teased, pulling Sami close to him.

Sami blushed slightly and looked up into his moss green eyes. "Someone might see us."

"We're the only ones here."

"You sure? I didn't see Ted leave."

"He had a dinner meeting with an agent from the Elite modeling agency. He left by five." Bruce loosened his grip on her. He reached over and flicked on the radio. It was set to the local Top 40 radio station. As the sound of Shakira's newest single filled the room, Bruce's eyes grew small and questioning. "Maybe you'd rather hear some Beethoven?" he asked.

"This is fine," Sami replied, avoiding his gaze.

"Well, you seemed so excited about going to that concert with that carpenter . . . what's his name?"

"Vin."

"Oh, right," Bruce continued. He stopped for a moment. "Did he hit on you?"

Sami shook her head. "Oh, no. It's nothing like that. He's just a friend. He doesn't think of me that way."

"Don't bet on it," Bruce told her. "You're so naive."

Sami's eyes flew open. "I am not."

"Oh, come on, Sami. You're such a trusting kid."

"I'm not a kid. And I'm a good judge of people. Vin is my friend. *Just* my friend."

Bruce reached over and pulled Sami close. "Well, see that it stays that way. Because I don't want anyone trying anything with my girlfriend."

Sami looked up at him with surprise. "Your *girlfriend*?"

"Sure," Bruce told her. "Didn't you feel it on Saturday? We're meant to be, Sami. It's kismet."

"But you've only known me a couple of weeks."

Bruce ran his fingers across her cheek. "I knew it the minute you walked in here. All sweetness and light, and nervous as hell. I said to myself, *There she is, Bruce. That's the girl you've been waiting for.*" He sighed gently. "Sometimes you just know it, Sami."

Sami didn't—couldn't—speak. The idea that Bruce had felt it, too, was just so overpowering. Instead, she stared into Bruce's eyes, hoping her own eyes would communicate the joy she felt.

Bruce kissed her lightly and then looked down at the portfolio sitting on the conference table. "Well, this isn't what we're here to talk about. I think we're here to get your career moving."

Sami nodded and unzipped the portfolio. "Do you want to see summer or winter first?" she asked him.

"I guess summer," he replied. "That's where my mind is, since that's what Ted's been working on these days."

Sami flipped the big pages until she came to a sketch of a summer suit that featured an asymmetrically hemmed cream-colored skirt and a black-and-cream blouse that laced across the chest. It was simple, but Sami felt it had a certain flair that made it stand out from the crowd.

"Hmm. Interesting," Bruce said in a noncommittal way. "And what material do you see the skirt made of?"

"I thought maybe a brushed cotton that

looks like suede. So it has sort of a south-western look, without being heavy," Sami replied cautiously.

Bruce nodded and turned the page. He looked carefully at the design—a black A-line dress with the added excitement of a lace bodice that gave the appearance of showing far more than it really did.

"Lots of women look good in A-lines," Sami explained. "But they're usually so matronly. I thought the lace made it more fun."

"It does," Bruce agreed. He turned the pages and looked at a few more of Sami's designs, stopping at a pink-and-white gingham ankle-length sleeveless dress. "This is interesting," he said.

"That's one of my favorites too," Sami said excitedly. "It's kind of playful, but you could wear it to the office. Well, not a Wall Street office, but just about any other kind. It makes you feel young and fresh but still look professional. See, I have another one that has sort of the same feel." She turned the page and showed him another dress, this one made of denim, with cap sleeves and a little fringe at the bottom of the skirt.

Bruce studied the picture carefully. "Hmm . . . ," he mused slowly. "You know, this is what Ted is going for—mixing work and play. Maybe I could show him these two."

Sami practically jumped out of her seat. "Bruce, would you really?"

"Hey, calm down." He laughed. "I'll show them to him. But that's no guarantee."

"I know," Sami agreed. "But it's a shot. And even if he doesn't like them, maybe he'd have some comments for me. I could learn a lot from him. He's got such good taste."

"And you taste awfully good," Bruce teased, kissing her hard on the mouth and running his hand through her hair.

The passion was overwhelming—like a short circuit between live wires that sent sparks flying through the room. Within seconds Sami found herself lying on the boardroom table with Bruce beside her, his hands gripping her body while his tongue searched hungrily for hers. Sami felt herself melting at his touch, her body experiencing things she'd never even imagined before. She was drowning in the taste of his mouth and the ferociousness of his touch. There was an uncontrollable hunger flowing from his body into hers. It seemed the more they clung to each other, the greater the hunger became.

For a moment, a flash of fear went through her. She'd never done anything like this before. And she wasn't certain she was ready for what Bruce so obviously had in mind.

"Bruce, I . . ." Sami was shocked at how far away her voice sounded. "I don't know if . . . I mean I've never . . . before . . ."

Bruce lifted his face from hers and looked into her eyes. "Never?" he said, surprised.

Sami blushed furiously and shook her head.

"We don't have to do anything you don't want to."

But Sami did want to. She'd never before had any desire to sleep with the boys that she knew in high school. Not even Billy Morrison, whom she'd dated for at least three months and had gone to the senior prom with.

But now, here, with this man, she was incapable of stopping herself—even if she'd wanted to. They barely knew each other, and yet, Sami was convinced he was her soul mate. Theirs was an understanding that had happened immediately. Sami had read about it many times. Bruce had called it kismet. Others called it love at first sight. No matter what name you gave this relationship, Sami was absolutely and unequivocally convinced that it was cosmic fate that they would wind up together.

Still, even as her body began to give way, Sami's mind stayed sharp enough to know that she didn't want to wind up like Celia. "But I don't have any . . . any protection," she murmured. "I don't want to . . ."

"Relax," Bruce assured her. "I have what we need. I would never let anything happen to you, Sami. Don't you know that? I want to protect you. Keep you safe." He reached into his pocket and pulled out a slim black leather wallet. Inside was a single condom, still in its blue wrapper.

Sami looked at him strangely. "You planned on—"

He shook his head. "I didn't plan this," he assured her. "I just hoped. I've been hoping. Ever since I met you, Sami, I haven't thought of anything else but you and me, like this. I have to admit that the boardroom wasn't quite the atmosphere I had in mind, but at the moment—"

Just then, Sami heard the loud bell that signaled the elevator opening on the floor. Then she heard footsteps entering the reception area. Her face turned beet red. Quickly, she sat up straight and took a deep breath. "Someone's coming," she whispered to Bruce.

"Damn," Bruce murmured. "The janitor."

"We'd better go," Sami suggested.

"He'll just think we're having a meeting," Bruce replied with certainty. "He'll be gone in a minute."

But the mood had been broken, and they both knew it. Sami slid off the table and hurried to find her shoes.

It was very late when Sami arrived back at her apartment. Ordinarily, Rain would have been awake, hanging out with her usual crowd of pierced and tattooed waiters and waitresses from the restaurant. But tonight, everything was dark and quiet. These days Rain made sure she went to bed right after her shift. She was determined to be in the best shape possible for the Mollie Mack show. And that meant early to bed and then early to rise for a complete work-out in the morning.

Sami was glad Rain was asleep. She didn't feel much like talking to anyone. So much had happened tonight. It was hard to believe that if that janitor hadn't shown up when he had, Sami might have—no, *would* have—slept with Bruce Jamison. She'd been so caught up in the moment that she was sure she would have gone through with it.

Part of her was disappointed that it hadn't happened. But an even bigger part of her was secretly relieved. Deep down, Sami knew that she and Bruce weren't ready to make that big of a step. And once they slept together there would be no turning back. Nothing would ever be the same between them again. Some people could do these things casually. But Sami Granger wasn't one of them. She hoped Bruce wasn't either.

She went into the kitchen, grabbed herself a soda, and went into the living room. As she sat there alone in the darkness, she forced her mind to go back to the boardroom. What was it Bruce had called their meeting? Oh yeah, *kismet*. That was it. What a perfect word. Filled with magic and joy.

She wrapped her arms around herself, remembering how it had felt to have Bruce there beside her. By now, the feeling of electric excitement of their passionate kisses was gone. In its place was a warm glow that enveloped her like a blanket.

For a moment, Sami thought about calling Celia and telling her everything that had happened. That was how it had always been. As Celia put it, there were no secrets between best friends. But the desire to kiss and tell everything to her sister-in-law passed quickly. She didn't really want to hear Celia tell her that she should have stayed with Bruce and waited for the janitor to leave. Sami had no doubt that that would be Celia's advice. But to tell the truth, her relationship with Bruce was one subject Sami didn't really want advice on. Not even from her best friend. These were decisions she would have to make on her own.

Nine

Despite getting to sleep so late, Sami had no trouble hopping out of bed the next morning. She was anxious to get to the office early, hoping for a little private time with Bruce before the craziness of the day set in. She dressed quickly and poured herself a cup of coffee.

Rain was already in the kitchen, drinking one of her healthful concoctions. "Coffee? For breakfast?" she said disdainfully. "You'll get more energy from this carrot avocado and spinach juice. It's got a little Tabasco—that'll give you the jump start you need."

Sami wrinkled her nose. "No thanks. I

think I'll stick with the coffee and some toast."

"Suit yourself," Rain said, sipping her drink. "So, you got in late. How'd it go with the great Mr. Jamison?"

Sami's eyes flew open. "Go?" she asked nervously. "With what?"

"With your designs," Rain said. "Did he like them?"

"Oh, my designs," Sami gulped.

"What else?" Rain asked suspiciously.

"Nothing," Sami replied, a tad too quickly. "He liked them. He's going to show them to Ted."

Rain poured herself more juice. "Okay. We'll see. I hope he's as good as his word."

"You don't like Bruce, do you?" Sami asked her.

"It's not that I don't like him. He's very charming," Rain began, obviously choosing her words carefully. "It's just that there are a lot of men out there, Sami, and I'd hate for you to fall for the first guy who flashes a little cash in your direction."

"You sound like Vin," Sami told her.

"You've discussed this with Vin?" Rain sounded surprised.

"Sure. He worries about me too. But you guys don't have to be so concerned. I'm a good judge of character. I can tell that Bruce really believes in me. Why else would he spend so much time with me, and offer to take my designs to Ted Fromme?"

"That's just what I was thinking," Rain mused.

"Oops, look at the time!" Sami hopped out of her chair and put her cup in the sink. "I'm going to be late for work if I don't get out of here."

"You going to be around tonight?" Rain called after her. "A bunch of us are going to dinner at Hunan Garden. Wanna come?"

"I think I'll be with Bruce tonight," Sami said.

"Oh, where's he taking you? Some place expensive, no doubt."

Sami frowned. That was the second time this morning that Rain had made some comment about Bruce's money. It was like she was prejudiced against people with money. Bruce happened to work very hard for what he had. Sami thought it was nice that Bruce was willing to spend it so freely on her. But there wasn't time to argue that with Rain, and besides, she really didn't want there to be any trouble between her and her roommate. So she simply replied, "I don't know where we'll go. We don't have anything planned."

"Then how do you know he's free?"

Sami smiled. "I just know it."

Bruce was already in his cubicle hard at work when Sami arrived. She was surprised. Ordinarily she was the first one in and he was the last.

"Wow! Look who's up with the sun," Sami chirped, sneaking into his cubicle, coming up behind him, and giving him a peck on the cheek.

Bruce jumped up, startled. He slammed the top of his laptop shut and turned to Sami. "Don't do that," he scolded her.

"There's no one else here," Sami promised. She leaned over and hugged his neck.

"I mean sneak up on me," Bruce continued, wriggling free from her playful grip. "You scared the heck out of me."

"I'm sorry," Sami apologized easily. She

wrapped her arms around his neck. "Let me make it up to you."

Bruce shook his head. "We can't do this here. Not now. People will be coming in any minute." He looked into her eyes, making sure she understood the importance of what he was saying. "No one can know about us."

"Is it against office rules?" Sami asked, suddenly nervous.

Bruce shook his head. "I don't know. But it wouldn't look good. Technically, I'm your boss, right? We don't need one of those Monica-Bill scandals around here."

Sami thought there was a big difference between a relationship between an office manager and a receptionist and one involving the president of the United States and an intern, but she could see that Bruce wasn't going to accept that kind of logic. "I guess you're right," she agreed, her face falling.

Bruce must've noted the sadness in her eyes, because he gave her one of his remarkable smiles. "But that doesn't mean we can't meet somewhere *after* work."

"That's true," Sami agreed. "Actually,

Rain and some of her friends are going out to dinner tonight at a local Chinese place. Do you want to go?"

Bruce heaved a heavy sigh. "Gee, Sam, I don't think so," he said slowly.

Sami studied his face. "Don't you like Rain?" she asked him.

"Sure, she's fine," Bruce said. "And I like her taste in roommates."

Sami smiled. "Then what's the problem?"

"I met a lot of people like Rain when I first came to New York. You know, all into the excitement and rebellion of the East Village," Bruce explained. "I've moved on from that East Village scene. You'll see. After you've been here a while, tattoos, tongue piercings, and pitchers of beer will lose their appeal. Besides, I was thinking you and I could go out alone tonight. How about La Comida?"

Sami knew all about La Comida. It was one of the new hot spots in town, and always crowded with celebrities. "Are you sure we can get in?"

"Do you doubt me?" Bruce asked her in mock horror.

"Never," Sami assured him. "I trust you completely."

"That's my girl," Bruce said. "Now get out of here. I have work to do. And I want to see if Ted can meet with me today to look at some of those designs you showed me last night."

"Ooo, I wish you hadn't told me that," Sami replied. "Now I'll be nervous all day."

"You have nothing to be nervous about," Bruce assured her. "Not as long as I'm in your corner."

But Sami couldn't help but be nervous as the day went on. Each time Ted Fromme walked past her desk, she waited anxiously for him to say something to her about her designs. When he didn't mention them, Sami was left to analyze his moods as he walked through the reception area. Did that smile mean he liked her sketches, or was he just being friendly? Or, why did he seem so distracted as he walked out the door to his lunch meeting? Was he deliberately avoiding her eyes because he didn't want to tell her he didn't like her work?

The suspense was killing her.

Then, at the very end of the day, just as he was leaving the office for the night, Ted Fromme stopped at Sami's desk—something he rarely did. Sami's heart began to beat so quickly, she was certain it would pop out of her chest any second. "Hi, Ted!" she greeted him, her voice cracking ever so slightly.

"You're here awfully late," Ted remarked in his slow, Southern drawl.

"Well, I have a few more things to do before I leave," Sami lied. Actually she was waiting for Bruce, but she knew she had to heed his warning about keeping their relationship under wraps.

"Well, don't work too hard," Ted said. "This city's full of adventure. You should go get yourself some."

And that was it. He turned and left the office. With absolutely no mention of Sami's designs. Her heart fell. Did that mean he didn't like them? Or that Bruce hadn't gotten a chance to show them to him? For a moment, Sami thought about running over to Bruce's cubicle and asking him what had happened in his meeting with Ted. But she thought better of it. Bruce was doing her a favor, after all. She didn't want to bug him about it. Besides, Bruce knew how important this was to her. If he had anything to tell her, he surely would.

Sami sat at her desk working until everyone had gone. Everyone except Bruce, anyway. When seven o'clock rolled around, he was still in his cubicle, hunched over his laptop. Sami picked up her phone and dialed his extension.

"Hello," he answered in the professional tone he reserved for the office.

"Mr. Jamison, I believe your dinner date is waiting for you in the reception area," Sami said playfully.

"Really?" Bruce's voice changed as he teased. "Listen, um, this is sort of a blind date. Can you tell me what she's like?"

Sami giggled slightly, and then decided to play along. "Oh, she's incredibly smart. And positively gorgeous," she told him. "In fact, if I didn't know better, I'd say she was a model."

"Oh, heaven forbid," Bruce said, laughing. "Models aren't my type at all. Listen, how about if I stand up this mystery woman and take you to dinner instead?"

"Just give me ten minutes to freshen up," Sami agreed.

"Great. I'll finish up here and meet you at the elevator."

La Comida was even more beautiful than Sami had read in the newspapers and magazines. From the moment you stepped inside you felt as though you had taken a trip in time back to old Spain. The scents of exotic spices filled the air. Each table was decorated with a hand-embroidered tablecloth topped with small white floating candles and fresh Spanish roses. Latin music played discreetly from hidden speakers, adding to the ambience without being obtrusive.

The clientele was impressive as well. Ever since La Comida had been crowned the new hot spot, all sorts of young celebrities and pseudo celebrities had been making the scene there. Sami had read that Leonardo DiCaprio had been there every night for a month while he was shooting his last film, and that Liv Tyler had celebrated her birthday in the VIP room.

Those celebs weren't there tonight, but

there was certainly enough glitter and glam to go around. In the corner, Sami recognized the faces of several young models she'd seen in fashion magazines and on TV commercials. Some were exotic, with long dark hair and unique features, while others had blond hair and blue eyes. But they were all long legged, and dressed magnificently in casual chic dresses and simple accessories. They giggled loudly, knowing they were bringing attention to themselves as they happily shared a single flan dessert.

Then Sami noticed a familiar face standing by the bar. "Oh, my goodness!" she squealed as she gripped Bruce's arm. "Isn't that Lucy Liu? It could be her, you know. I read somewhere that she was born in New York. . . ." Sami's eyes suddenly fell on another woman at the bar. She was a tall, beautiful African-American woman with long, dyed blond hair. Her clothes were obviously very expensive, if a little flashy. There was a crowd around her, and by the looks of her flamboyant hand motions, she enjoyed that immensely. She was the most exotic woman Sami'd ever seen.

Or is she? "Oh wow!" Sami exclaimed suddenly. "That's a *man!*"

"For God's sake, Sami, don't stare," Bruce hissed in her ear. "And don't talk so loud."

Sami blushed. She hadn't realized that she'd been staring or shouting. She'd just been so shocked by the realization.

"That's not just any man," Bruce whispered. "It's **RuPaul**, a very famous entertainer."

"I've never heard of her . . . or should I say him . . . I mean, what do you call him or her?"

Bruce rolled his eyes. "RuPaul."

Sami nodded. "Boy, wait until I tell Celia about this."

"For God's sake, Sami, stop behaving like a tourist. Keep your cool. Just act like you're one of them."

Sami looked at Bruce as though he had three heads. How could she—a girl from Elk Lake, Minnesota—ever pretend to be one of the beautiful New York people? It wasn't possible.

Bruce went up to the mâitre d' and gave him his name. The man looked skeptical at first, but then checked his list. "Ah, here you are, *Señor* Jamison. Right this way."

They followed the man to a table far in the back, not far from the bathrooms. Still, Sami was thrilled just to be in the restaurant. Bruce, however, was not happy. "Don't you have anything better?" he demanded.

"I'm sorry, *señor,* but we're totally booked for tonight. This is our last table."

Bruce sighed heavily.

"It's okay," Sami insisted. "I've got a great view of the restaurant from here."

"It'll have to do," Bruce said finally.

A few moments later, a waiter appeared, and Bruce ordered dinner for the both of them, since Sami seemed confused by the menu. "Just trust me," Bruce told Sami before he told the waiter what to bring. "I wouldn't steer you wrong."

Sami nodded and sipped on her water. She was trying to look nonchalant and sophisticated, just as Bruce had urged her to do. But the truth was, she was nervous and excited, waiting for Bruce to bring up the topic of her designs.

He didn't. They exchanged small talk throughout the meal, chatting about New

York things: how awful the subways were, whether the mayor's ban on smoking would ruin the club scene, and the high cost of rent. Not once did either of them mention anything having to do with the office. Most of the time it was Bruce holding forth with his opinions. Sami had nothing to compare these situations to. So she just nodded a lot. *Like my dad taught me,* she realized.

Finally, after a full meal of chicken and rice, Sami couldn't hold herself back any longer. "Bruce," she asked. "Did you get a chance to talk to Ted about my designs?"

Bruce nodded and took a long sip of his sangria. Then he leaned back in his chair. "I was hoping not to talk about that until we'd finished dinner," he said slowly.

Sami knew from his expression that the news wasn't good. "He didn't like them very much, did he?"

"It's not that he didn't like them, Sami; in fact, he thought some of your ideas were good. But the execution was just a little amateurish."

Amateurish. The word cut like a knife. "B-b-but you said they were good. You liked them so much," she blubbered as she struggled not to cry.

Bruce took her hand in his. "Well, you have to admit that I'm a little biased when it comes to anything having to do with you." He smiled warmly at her. "Besides, Ted said they showed promise. They just needed some fine tuning. Come on, that's more than most get to hear from someone like Ted."

Sami shrugged. "I guess." She thought for a moment. "Look, what if I went to talk to him myself? I could even wear some of the dresses that I modeled on those designs. Maybe if I brought the whole thing to life . . . He did like the neck on that blouse I made, and—"

"No, don't do that," Bruce warned her urgently.

"Why not? It's worth a try."

"It'll just make Ted angry," Bruce told her. "He's a busy man. He's not concerned with your feelings. If you make a big deal out of this, he'll never look at anything you've got ever again. Trust me. This best thing to do is wait a few months and then show him something else."

Sami blinked, fighting back the tears.

She didn't want to cry. Not here, in this fabulous restaurant. Not after Bruce had been so wonderful about helping her . . . even if it hadn't worked out the way they'd hoped.

Bruce put down his wineglass and stared into her eyes. "Look, this isn't the end of the world. You've got what it takes. You just need a little more experience. Maybe you could take a class at FIT. I'll bet the company would pay for part of it."

Classes. Back to school . . . "I'll think about it."

Bruce nodded sympathetically. "I guess you don't want any dessert now."

"I've kind of lost my appetite," Sami told him.

Bruce called over the waiter and quickly paid the check. Then he escorted Sami outside and reached out his arm for a cab.

"Riverside and Eighty-second," he told the driver as they climbed into the taxi.

"Where are we going?" Sami asked him.

"I thought we'd go back to my place," Bruce said. "It's more private there than at your apartment."

"Bruce, I don't know. Maybe I should just go home."

He stared at her with surprise. "What? You're only into me if I can help you with Ted?" he teased, but something in his voice sounded . . . demanding.

Sami was surprised. "No, that's not it at all. I'm just tired and a little disappointed."

"Look, we don't have to do anything. I just thought you could use a little luxury tonight—instead of going back into that walk-up building and crashing in that little bed of yours. I promise I'll cheer you up," he declared as he leaned over and gave her a hard kiss on the lips.

But Sami knew nothing could cheer her up. And sex with Bruce was probably the furthest thing from her mind. "I really need to go home," she told him, choking back the tears.

Ten

Sami didn't sleep well that night. Her disappointment was overwhelming—as was the fear that Bruce was going to lose interest in her because she'd refused to go home with him the night before. Of course he'd said all the right things, assuring her that he understood and walking her to the door. But Sami thought she heard something change in his voice. It was more than just disappointment. He'd suddenly sounded as though he were speaking to a naive young girl rather than to the woman he called his girlfriend.

Since sleeping was obviously out of the question, Sami got out of bed just before sunrise and decided to take a shower and have a cup of coffee, hoping that would be enough to keep her awake through the day.

Rain awoke just after six and emerged from the bedroom just as Sami was putting another top on her cup of coffee.

"I'll take one of those if you're pouring," Rain murmured, wiping the sleep from her eyes.

Sami nodded and pulled down a second mug. She looked over at Rain. It was amazing how great her roommate could look first thing in the morning, even with her tousled red hair and makeup-free face. She was just one of those natural-born beauties.

Of course Sami had thought she was a natural-born designer. But that was before Ted Fromme had pulled the rug out from under her dreams. She sighed heavily and finished her cup of coffee, then dragged herself into the bedroom. She was grateful that Rain was too tired to start up a conversation over coffee. Sami didn't feel much like talking.

Quickly she went into her small closet and pulled out a blue-green linen dress that brought out her eyes. She studied her face in the mirror as she put on a little mascara and some lip gloss. Then she headed out the door and prepared to make her way through the crowds on the subway platform to board the train that would take her to work. As a *receptionist.*

Sami let out a blasé sigh. Nothing about New York seemed very exciting anymore.

"So did you take my advice?" Ted Fromme asked Sami as he walked into the office just a few minutes after she had arrived.

"Your advice?" she said. "You mean about FIT?"

"What about FIT?" Ted asked.

Sami shook her head. Come to think of it, it had been Bruce who had suggested the schooling, not Ted. "Nothing," she murmured.

"I meant about going out and seeing the town," Ted continued.

"Well, I went to La Comida last night with . . . a . . . uh . . . friend," Sami told him, keenly recalling Bruce's warning about the importance of keeping their relationship a secret.

"Nice friend," Ted said. "That place is great. I used to go there quite a lot when it first opened. Now I've moved on to Cafe 17. You know how it is in New York: The hot spots keep changing."

Just then, Bruce strolled into the office. His face fell slightly when he caught a glimpse of Sami talking to Ted. He walked over and stopped in front of her desk. "Any messages for me?"

"Oh, Bruce, just the man I wanted to see," Ted greeted him. "How are those designs coming?"

"You'll have them by Friday morning, I promise," Bruce assured him.

"I hope so," Ted replied. "You're the last of the junior designers to submit his designs."

Sami could see Bruce's shoulders sag at the way Ted emphasized the word "junior." It was hard for a man as dedicated and ambitious as Bruce to think of himself as a junior anything.

"You'll have them," Bruce reassured him. "I just want to put in a few extras to make sure these are the designs that blow you away."

Ted nodded and smiled slightly. "I'll see you later, Sami," he said as he walked away. "I'm glad you considered my advice."

Bruce waited until Ted was gone before he perched himself on the corner of Sami's desk and studied her face carefully. "What advice was that?" he asked with a curious tone in his voice.

"Oh, he just told me to go out and enjoy myself more. I told him I was at La Comida last night. But don't worry, I just said I went with a friend."

"You didn't talk to him about the designs?" Bruce asked anxiously.

"No, and he didn't mention them, either," Sami said mournfully. "I think he has a heart of steel. How can he be so nice to my face after rejecting my designs?"

"That's just Ted," Bruce said quickly. "He doesn't think he did anything to hurt your feelings. To him, it's just business."

"But he must have been an aspiring designer at some point. He must remember how that felt."

Bruce shrugged. "That was a few years and several million dollars ago, Sami."

"I guess."

"He was right about you getting out to see the city more, though," Bruce said, changing the subject. "The excitement suits you." He chuckled. "I don't think I'll ever forget your face when you saw RuPaul. It was classic!"

Sami blushed.

"There are so many hot spots in this city. We'll get to all of them," Bruce continued.

"I know," Sami agreed. "And not all of them are so expensive. Vin told me about this place in the West Village where the waiters sing opera."

"*Vin* recommended it?" Bruce noted. There was that tone again, she realized.

"Do you want to try it?" Sami asked, consciously ignoring the tone in his voice. "We could go tonight."

"*Sami,*" Bruce warned her.

"What? No one heard me. There's no one here but us." She was right. The reception area was empty.

"Yes, but someone might walk in," Bruce reminded her.

"I'm sorry," Sami apologized.

Bruce smiled warmly. "It's okay. Working

together like this is hard for me, too. Sometimes I have to fight off the urge to just run out here and grab you in the middle of the day. You look awfully sexy answering those phones, you know."

Sami laughed. "You should see me when I sign for a package."

"I'll be picturing it all day," Bruce assured her. "Believe me, I'd love to do anything with you—even go to some place Vin recommended. Unfortunately, tonight's impossible. You heard Ted. I have to get those designs finished by Friday. But after that, I'm all yours. Maybe we can go out Saturday night and celebrate."

"Okay, you put out the paper plates, and I'll get the chicken," Sami told Rain later that night, when the two girls were alone in their apartment.

"I'm so psyched. I haven't had a home-cooked meal since . . . since I left home," Rain said as she set the kitchen table. "Unless of course you count the endless boxes of mac and cheese I've shoved down my throat since I moved here."

"I thought it would be fun," Sami said

as she checked the chicken one last time to make sure it was cooked. "I hope you like this. It's a recipe my dad uses at the coffee shop. It's usually the Wednesday special. Of course, he makes it with mashed potatoes on the side, but since you're getting ready for Mollie Mack, I thought grilled veggies would be better."

"Sounds yummy." Rain watched her roommate carefully. Sami hadn't said anything about how Bruce's meeting with Ted Fromme had gone, but Rain had a feeling that Sami wouldn't be home making chicken if he'd suddenly declared her the next Coco Chanel. Still, Rain hadn't wanted to pry into Sami's business. If she wanted to talk about it, Rain figured she would.

Just as Sami placed the chicken on the table, there was a knock at the door. Three short taps and one loud pound.

"I'll get it," Rain told her as she leaped up to get the door. She unhooked the chain, turned the two bolt locks, and clicked the small latch over the doorknob to the right before she could open the door.

"Hey, don't you ask who it is first?" Vin asked as he faced Rain in the doorway.

"I recognized your knock," Rain assured him. "What's that?"

She pointed to the dark brown table Vin carried in his arms.

"It's for Sami," Vin said, placing the table down in the living room.

"I've been living across the hall from you for a year now and I've never once gotten anything more than a curtain rod. Sami's here a few days and she gets this?" Rain teased.

Vin blushed slightly.

"Ooh, I've struck a nerve." Rain laughed. Then she called into the kitchen, "Sami, come here. You've got to see this!"

"What's up?" Sami asked as she came out of the kitchen. "Hey, Vin. What's doing?"

"It's what *Vin's* been doing," Rain said as she pointed to the beautiful wooden table. "Making this for you."

Vin pointed at the table. "It's a drafting table. I thought you might need it now that you're working at Ted Fromme."

Sami walked over and ran her fingers over the smooth, lightly stained wood. Vin had constructed the table so that the top could be tilted at different angles. There were spaces for pens, and rulers, and other tools a designer might use. At the top he'd gracefully carved the letters "SG," her initials. It was the most beautiful thing Sami had ever seen.

Suddenly, the tears she'd been holding in for the past twenty-four hours came crashing out of her body like a tidal wave.

Vin stared at her with surprise. "Not exactly the reception I was expecting. Is something wrong?"

Sami shook her head. "It's beautiful," she told him through her tears. "I just wish I could use it. I don't think I'll be doing much designing anymore."

It took Vin a minute to figure out what Sami meant. As it became clear, he walked over and gently draped his arm around her, and let the tears flow onto his shoulder. After a moment he said, "Don't stop drawing just because of one guy's opinion. He's only a junior designer."

Sami shook her head. "It wasn't Bruce. It was Ted Fromme."

"Bruce actually showed your designs to him?" Rain asked with surprise.

"Of course," Sami told her. "He said he would. But it doesn't matter, because Ted didn't like them. He said my work was amateurish."

"Ted Fromme told you that?" Vin asked.

"Well, not exactly. But that's what he told Bruce, and——"

Vin's body tensed. *"Bruce . . . ,"* he started with a quiet anger. "So you didn't actually speak to Ted Fromme."

Sami shrugged. "What does it matter? I got the message. Ted Fromme doesn't think my stuff is professional enough."

"What does Ted Fromme know?" Rain butted in. "He may be today's news, but you're tomorrow's big star. Someday he'll be begging you for work! Then you can tell *him* he's an amateur!" She pounded her fist on the desk for emphasis.

"Hey, take it easy," Vin warned, rubbing his hand lovingly over the hand-carved wood. "It's not made of titanium, you know."

Sami stared at Rain with surprise. Her outburst was so intense that Sami couldn't help but laugh. "You guys are the best," she said.

Rain nodded. "You know it."

"Common knowledge," Vin added.

"No, I mean it," Sami said. "I was about to give up on drawing."

"Oh, we'd never let you do that," Vin assured her.

Rain came up beside Sami and put her arm around her so that the three of them were all standing side by side. "We take care of one another," she told Sami.

"Like family," Vin suggested.

Rain shook her head. "Nah. We're better than family. We're the Three Musketeers. One for all and all for one."

Sami sniffed at the air. The scent of herbed chicken was very powerful. "Vin, you'll stay, won't you? There's plenty of food."

Vin looked at Rain. "She cooks, too?"

Rain nodded. "She's a woman of many talents, our Sami."

Vin watched as Sami walked toward the kitchen. "Tell me about it," he agreed. Then, as soon as she was out of earshot, he whispered to Rain, "Where's Bruce? Shouldn't he be consoling her?"

Rain shrugged. "I think he's busy with

his own work. Sami said she wasn't going to see him until Saturday."

Vin frowned. "That guy's a piece of work."

Eleven

As it turned out, Sami never got to see Bruce that weekend.

She'd waited for him to mention something on Friday, but he was in meetings with Ted Fromme the whole day, and they never got to speak. On Saturday, she sat with her mind so focused on the phone that Rain teased her mercilessly that her ear would drop off if she stretched it any farther. But there was still no call from Bruce. Rain had suggested that Sami call him if she wanted to talk to him so badly. But Sami was forced to admit that he'd never given her his phone number. Sami tried hard to ignore the fact that Rain wasn't surprised to hear that.

By the time Sami got to work on Monday there was an awful feeling in the pit of her stomach that something was terribly wrong. Bruce didn't make her feel any better when he arrived at the office early Monday morning. He breezed past Sami's desk with barely a hello. Sami had smiled and tried to catch his attention, but Bruce's mind seemed focused elsewhere.

Sami didn't have long to bemoan the fact that Bruce seemed to be ignoring her. Ted Fromme arrived at the office at 9:00 A.M. He seemed exceptionally excited.

"Sami, please send out an e-mail to the entire staff. I need everyone in the boardroom at 10:00 A.M. sharp for a staff meeting. That means you, too. I have a big announcement, and I think it's one you'll want to hear."

"Really?"

Ted laughed. "Don't think you can get it out of me by batting those big blue eyes," he teased. "It's a surprise. "

By the time ten o'clock rolled around, everyone who worked at Ted Fromme

Fashions had come up with his or her own theory about what the meeting would be about.

"Do you think Ted has merged with Ralph Lauren?" Suzi in accounting wondered. "There was that rumor going around."

"I heard it was with Tommy Hilfiger," Emma, a secretary in the marketing department, countered.

"Maybe he's bringing in a big-name designer to spruce up the spring line," suggested Jackson from sales.

"Do you think he's opening a European office?" Justine, one of the junior designers, asked hopefully. "I would love to work in Paris, or maybe Milan."

"You don't think he's closing us down, do you?" Alex, the computer tech expert, asked nervously. "I just bid on a co-op in Park Slope."

As Ted strolled into the giant conference room at 10:00 on the dot, it was easy to see that he enjoyed the suspense his call for a meeting had created. While Ted walked to the front of the room, his ever present cup of coffee in hand, Sami searched the conference room looking for Bruce, even though she knew instinctively that he wasn't there yet. She'd developed a kind of sixth sense where Bruce was concerned: She could feel his presence when he entered a room.

Finally, Bruce appeared in the doorway. He stood there for a moment, his arms filled with large pieces of sketch paper. When he was certain that all eyes were upon him, Bruce entered the room, strutting toward Ted.

Sami blushed as Bruce placed the sketches on a large easel and sat leisurely on top of the conference table, his arms folded nonchalantly across his chest. It was the exact same pose he'd taken that night when they'd stayed late together. She wondered if Bruce was remembering the same thing. But as she looked across the room she didn't spot any glimmer of remembrance in Bruce's moss-green eyes. Instead, she got the distinct impression he was avoiding her glance, focusing on Ted instead.

"Okay, boys and girls," Ted called out in a voice that wasn't very loud. Ted had a habit of speaking softly at meetings.

Interestingly enough, his low tone had a much stronger effect than a loud, booming voice. People automatically quieted down when he spoke, focusing on his every word to make sure that they heard him correctly. "I'll end your suspense right now. As you know, we've been looking for some fresh designs for our new show. And I've found them. I'd like you all to be the first to witness the Bruce Jamison line, specially designed for Ted Fromme Fashions!"

Sami gasped. Ted was giving Bruce his own line! *No wonder Bruce had been too busy to call me all weekend.* He and Ted had probably been in meetings the whole time. She smiled broadly, hoping her expression would show him just how excited and proud she felt.

"So, let's take a look, shall we?" Ted said, unveiling the first in a series of sketches. Sami turned her head, anxious to see what Bruce had come up with. She realized suddenly that he'd never once shown her his work. Now she would get a chance to see the kind of style Bruce was interested in.

What she saw made her stomach drop—and her blood pressure rise.

The sketch Ted had just displayed was of a pink-and-white gingham ankle-length sleeveless dress. It was Sami's dress—the one she'd shown Bruce that night in the boardroom!

"You see, this is what I've been looking for," Ted explained. "Bruce, how was it you described your line? Oh, yes. Clothes that will make women feel young and fresh, but still look professional."

Sami's heart was pounding wildly now. That was exactly how she'd described her designs to Bruce. He'd not only stolen her work, he'd stolen her words.

Ted flipped the page once again to show a cotton summer suit that featured an asymmetrically hemmed cream-colored skirt and a black-and-cream blouse that laced across the chest. "Now this design is incredibly unique, not just because of the look, but because of the fabric Bruce is considering."

"This one will look like suede, but it will really be made of brushed cotton, so it can have that Southwestern flair, without being heavy," Bruce explained.

He flipped the page to show Sami's black A-line dress with a lace bodice. "Almost every woman looks good in an A-line dress," Bruce continued, quoting what he'd heard Sami say. "This just adds a certain twist."

"I think this will be a big seller for us," Ted continued. "I'm thinking of putting it out there in several colors, maybe patterns, too. It could be as big as the wrap dress was in the seventies."

Sami couldn't believe what was happening. At first it was all too surreal to digest. But the realization came fast and furious: Bruce had stolen her designs, *every one of them.*

How could she have been so stupid? She'd trusted him, and the only truth he'd ever told her was that he'd shown the designs to Ted. Unfortunately, he'd passed them off as his own.

Suddenly, all the anger inside her boiled over. Sami couldn't control herself. "Those are mine!" she shouted out, right in front of everyone. "Bruce, tell him those designs are *mine!*"

Bruce stared at Sami as though he'd never seen her before. "I don't know what she's talking about," he swore to Ted.

"You *liar*! You asked me to show you my

portfolio, and then you stole my designs."

"Sami, what is the meaning of this?" Ted asked, his voice growing softer as his irritation became apparent.

"I designed those dresses, Ted. And lots more like them." She pointed to Bruce. "*He* told me you thought they were unprofessional."

"Sami, this isn't the time or place," Ted said calmly. "If you have some work you'd like to show me, we can make an appointment."

"I don't need an appointment," Sami insisted. "You've already seen my work. It's right there!"

A murmur ran through the room. Everyone was talking at once. "Okay, let's quiet down," Ted said. "The show's over. Go back to work. Bruce, can I see you in my office?"

For a moment, Sami thought that Ted believed her. But as she caught a glimpse of Bruce walking behind his boss, she knew in an instant that Bruce would never let that happen. He shot her an angry look that plainly broadcast his warning: *Don't try it. You're sure to lose.*

Sami had no doubt that was true. Bruce was a master at making people believe what he wanted them to. And there was no way he was going to lose his chance to be a big-name designer. Not for Sami . . . not for anyone. He'd simply tell Ted that she was a lunatic. Or that she was out to destroy him because they'd had a doomed love affair. Anything to save his own neck. And there was no doubt that Ted would believe him.

The others in the room weren't sure what to think. They glanced from Sami to Bruce and Ted leaving the room and then back to Sami again.

"You guys believe me, don't you?" Sami asked her coworkers.

No one knew what to say to her. It was obvious from the looks on their faces that they knew that Bruce Jamison was capable of almost anything. On the other hand, Bruce was the favorite son now. Sami knew that backing her would be career suicide for them.

She couldn't win. So, without even so much as a glance at the other people in the room, Sami stormed out and hurried to the reception area. She went back to her desk and began to pack up the few things she'd placed in her drawer. Her arms seemed to be moving on their own without any direction from her brain. She could no longer think, or feel much of anything. For the moment, her brain was protecting her from a pain that she couldn't handle right now. She gathered her personal items in her arms and walked toward the elevators. As she stood there waiting for the doors to open, her mind shifted back to that first day when she'd gotten the job. That woman— Roxie—had warned her that Ted Fromme Fashions was hell, and that Bruce Jamison was the devil himself.

Sami should have heeded the warning.

"I'm going to kill him!" Rain screeched when Sami arrived home about an hour later and poured out her tale. "How could anybody *do* that? He stole your work. That's sick!"

"He stole a lot more than that," Sami said sadly. "He stole my heart."

Rain reached over and put an arm around her roommate. "You really liked him, huh?"

Sami nodded. "I can't believe I was so stupid. He kept telling me to trust him, over and over again. And I did."

"There's no way you could make Ted Fromme believe you?" Rain asked. "I mean, show him some of your other designs?"

Sami shook her head. "By now, Bruce has him convinced that I belong in a mental hospital and that the company is better off rid of a child like me."

Vin had been sitting on the living room couch listening as Rain raved, and Sami spoke in a pained, numbed voice. He hadn't said a word until now. "You know, Sami, there is something good in all this . . . ," he began.

"Not now, Vin." Rain's eyes warned him not to gloat over the fact that he'd been right about Bruce Jamison.

"Not that," Vin assured her. "What Sami has to realize is that Ted Fromme *did* like her designs."

"But he thinks they're Bruce's," Sami insisted.

"Yeah, well, that's another conversation for another day," Vin said. "What you have to focus on is that obviously you do have what it takes to be a designer. You need to get back to work, Sami. Design something better than those dresses, and get a different design house to look at them."

Sami shook her head. "Who's going to look at my work? That was the problem I had when I first got here."

"Vin's right," Rain told her. "You have to get right back up on that design horse. Otherwise, Bruce Jamison comes out of this the winner."

Sami wasn't so sure. "So how am I supposed to pay the rent while I'm coming up with a new book of designs?"

Rain thought for a moment. "Well, you could take a day job. Something to tide you over while you work on your real career."

"You mean wait tables or something?" Sami asked her, perking up a bit. "I could do that. I've got tons of experience. I did it all the time at my dad's place. Do they need anyone at Dojo?"

Rain shook her head. "Not right now, but I'm sure—"

"Hey, wait a minute, isn't Lola looking for someone to work in her shop?" Vin interrupted.

Rain's eyes flew open. "Yeah! That would be perfect for you, Sami. You'd be around clothing all day, and then you could design at night."

"You mean at a boutique?" Sami asked.

Rain and Vin exchanged glances.

"Something like that," they both said at once.

It was a few weeks later when Sami finally picked up the phone and called Celia. She realized it had been almost a month since she'd spoken to her best friend. Celia had left a few messages, but Sami had been so busy that she'd never gotten to call her back. The thought that she'd been so wrapped up in Bruce that she'd neglected her best friend made her even more angry with him . . . and disappointed in herself.

"Hello?" Celia said as she picked up the phone.

"Hi, Celia," Sami said, quickly adding, "I'm so sorry I haven't called. It's been crazy, and I—"

"Oh, don't worry about it, kiddo. I know you've been busy. How's life at Ted Fromme?"

"I wouldn't know," Sami replied calmly.

"What are you talking about?" Celia asked.

"It turned out my boss was a real snake," Sami began. "He stole my designs." The words burned like bile as Sami relayed the whole bitter story of her romance with Bruce, and the deception she had endured at his hands. She finished her tale by telling Celia not to worry, that she had a new job at a shop in the East Village, so she would be able to pay her rent.

Celia listened quietly, managing to croon a "you poor baby" from time to time as Sami spoke. When she was certain that her best friend had said all she'd needed to, Celia took a deep breath. "I'm so sorry that your first love turned out to be a jerk," she said.

"He said I should trust him," Sami moaned.

"They all say that," Celia commiserated.

"Yeah, well, I'm never going to fall for that line again," Sami declared. "I'm never going to trust another man as long as I live. From now on, my nights are going to be spent at my drawing table. Did I tell you my friend Vin made me a drawing table? It's really gorgeous, dark wood and—"

"Don't change the subject," Celia said. "You've got to talk this thing out. It's the only way you're going to be able to move on."

"Uh-uh. No moving on. No more men, ever!"

"I know you feel that way now, Sami, but you'll get over him, I promise."

"No, I won't," Sami insisted. "From now on, I'm flying solo."

"You're willing to give designing another try, but not love?" Celia asked her. "That doesn't make any sense."

"It makes perfect sense," Sami replied. "My designs are all mine. They don't depend on anyone else. And I will never depend on anyone else again."

"But Sami, your designs can't keep you warm at night, they can't give you children—"

"Not everyone wants children, Celia," Sami snapped back. She stopped, surprised at the vehemence in her own voice. "Sorry, I didn't mean to say having children was a bad thing."

"I know," Celia answered gently. "You're still raw. I don't blame you. But Sami, someday—"

"No buts about it. I've learned my lesson. Anyway, enough about me." She struggled to change the subject, not wanting to argue with Celia any longer. "How are you, and my brother's future progeny, doing?"

"Oh, we're okay."

Something in Celia's voice alarmed Sami. "Just okay?"

"You know me too well." Celia sighed. "It's no big deal, and I don't want you to worry. It's just that my blood pressure was up a little this visit, and the doctor wants me to take it easy."

"Are you on bed rest?" Sami asked anxiously.

"No, nothing like that," Celia said. "But no more working out, not even pregnancy classes. And that means I'm going to be as big as a horse when this baby comes out."

"Oh, don't worry about that," Sami assured her, relieved that it was nothing more serious.

"Easy for you to say," Celia said. "You're walking around in little sundresses while I'll be in muumuus for the rest of the summer."

Sami giggled. "I think we can come up with something a little more stylish. I'll make you something. I just picked up a secondhand sewing machine really cheap."

"You'll need a lot of fabric."

"Celia, cut it out," Sami scolded her. "The important thing is that you take care of yourself and the baby. Weight's easy. You'll take it off quick."

"I know," Celia agreed. "I'm just feeling sorry for myself. Must be the hormones. Anyway, can we talk about something else, please?"

"We can't talk about the baby, and I don't want to hear another word about men," Sami mused. "What's left?"

"Oh, there must be something," Celia told her. "How about telling me about your work. You said your friends helped you get a job in a store. What kind of place is it?"

"It's a lingerie shop here in the Village."

"Ooo. I love lingerie," Celia cooed. "Is it like Victoria's Secret?"

"Something like that," Sami replied slowly.

"What's the name of the place?"

"Beneath the Sheets."

Twelve

Sami hadn't been exactly honest with Celia about Beneath the Sheets. At least not in the *tell the truth, the whole truth, and nothing but the truth* sense of the word. Yes, Beneath the Sheets did sell lingerie, but that was where the comparisons with places like Victoria's Secret ended. Beneath the Sheets also sold other items that were meant for the boudoir—things Sami had never seen before.

"What's this used for?" Sami asked Lola as she draped a feathery boa on a hook during her first week of work.

"Don't worry about that, hon," Lola had said in her gruff, smoke-tinged voice. "If a customer asks you for it, she'll know what to do with it."

Sami had blushed and gone over and rearranged the lace panties (some complete, some not so much), and had tried to make a display of teddies and baby doll pajamas that was both "pleasin' and teasin'," as Lola liked to say.

Sami had deliberately left out the more sordid side of Beneath the Sheets during her conversation with Celia. She'd had a feeling that her best friend wouldn't approve of her working in a place that sold the kind of merchandise that Lola made available for her customers. And if Al had found out—well, he'd have been on the next plane to New York, ready to drag Sami back to Elk Lake. Al and Celia weren't prudes, by any means, but Sami knew this wasn't the kind of shop either of them would ever step foot in. And that was just Al and Celia. Sami didn't even want to think about her father's reaction to all this.

In fact, Sami herself had been shocked when she'd first arrived to apply for a job at Beneath the Sheets. But after a couple of days, Sami had actually grown accustomed to the place. She consoled herself with the knowledge that at least she was able to be around clothing, even if it was just lingerie. And Lola gave Sami a lot of artistic freedom, asking her to design the window treatments for the shop, and to create displays inside the store. Sami spent hours at her new drafting table, laying out ideas for the displays. There was a certain creative excitement in being able to do that. And Lola's enthusiastic encouragement for her projects was a welcome salve for her bruised emotional well-being.

Sami loved working with Lola. She was what Sami's dad would call "a tough old broad." Lola was a genuine native of Greenwich Village, born in the 1950s and raised there during the height of the wild '60s hippie era. Lola was one of the last holdouts of a time gone by. She had a peace sign tattooed on her shoulder, and a yinyang on her back. She liked to play old Janis Joplin albums in the store, and still wore her long, gray frizzy hair in pigtails. Lola also took great pride in the fact that her bell-bottom jeans were totally vintage—and right from her own closet.

Lola told great tales about Greenwich Village, back when there were no McDonald's or Burger Kings on Bleecker Street, and musicians like Bob Dylan and Joan Baez used to hang out in Washington Square Park. Sami was convinced that the customers at Beneath the Sheets stopped in as much to listen to Lola tell stories of affairs she'd had with old folk stars as they did to buy lingerie. As Sami's dad would say, "Lola could sure spin a good story." Just like Mac Granger was known to do.

Lola wasn't all that different from Sami's dad, a fact that, once Sami really thought about it, could explain why she felt so comfortable and relaxed around Lola. Sure, Sami's dad was a lot more provincial than Lola—he certainly wouldn't have approved of her business. But, like Lola, Mac Granger was happiest right where he'd grown up. They were both sort of legends in their own small worlds. It was just that Lola's world was a section of New York City, and Mac's neighborhood was a small town in Minnesota. Sami could sense neither one of them felt comfortable when they ventured too far from home.

There were other similarities, as well. Mac was pretty tough, but he always listened to the troubles of the patrons who came into his coffee shop. He always said he was part shrink, part coffee pourer. And like Mac, Lola wasn't so tough that she couldn't provide a shoulder to cry on when a client had a romance gone wrong. She always knew just what to say about men who did their women wrong. "You know what it is about men," she'd say. "They all share a single brain. And if one of them is using it, the rest of them are just plain stupid until it's their turn."

It was amazing just how much the customers opened up to Lola about their romantic problems. They had no problem talking about their most intimate details with her. Sami remembered having been completely shocked the first day she'd worked there. A tall, well-dressed woman in a tan summer suit and carrying a briefcase had wandered into the shop. In a firm, calm, completely unembarrassed voice, she'd asked Lola, "Did you get the black teddie with the red hearts on it in yet?"

Lola had shaken her head. "Not yet. They're still on order."

"Oh, that's too bad," the woman had replied. "I thought it would be a fun surprise tonight. My husband and I need to spice things up a bit."

"Oh, if spice is what you want, try this," Lola had replied, handing the woman a container of cinnamon-flavored massage oil. "If it doesn't work, you can always pour it in your coffee. Ever had coffee with cinnamon in it? Delicious."

At the time, Sami had been surprised at how easily these two women had joked about men. But now, several weeks later, as she stacked the various bras on the shelves, she barely noticed what Lola and her current customer were chatting about.

"Hey, Sami, can you get Marisol here one of those blue teddies in an extra large?" Lola called out to her.

Sami looked curiously at Marisol. She was a big woman, with wide hips (well earned after having delivered four babies, as Marisol often joked) and several rolls in her midsection. Sami wasn't sure that a teddy would have the effect Marisol desired. She thought she might look sexier in a long, silky nightgown with plenty of lace across the chest, bringing the attention up to her considerable and remarkable cleavage. But the customer wanted a teddy, and it wasn't up to Sami to tell her otherwise.

Still, that didn't mean Sami couldn't make a suggestion—tactfully, of course. So when she came back from the stockroom, she was carrying both a blue teddy and a long, silky cream-colored nightgown with a very low-cut top.

"Here's the teddy," Sami told Marisol, "and I also brought out this." She held up the nightgown. "We just got them in. I love it. Leaves just enough to the imagination. I thought you might want to try it on too."

Completely agreeable, Marisol took both into the dressing room. Sami waited impatiently, trying to see if her subtle suggestion had hit its mark. A few minutes later, Marisol came out, clutching both pieces of lingerie. "I think I'll try both," Marisol said, placing the nightgown and the teddy on the counter. "Keep him guessing."

Lola rang up the sale and sent Marisol on her way. As the door closed behind

Marisol, Lola turned to Sami. "That was slick," she said. "You're a real natural. I think you were meant to work in lingerie."

Sami giggled. "I prefer working in jeans and a T-shirt."

Lola laughed. "Yeah. You might get arrested if you decided to work in some of the things we've got lyin' around here." She held up a pair of pink fur-trimmed panties and a matching bra.

"That's not really me," Sami told her.

"These aren't really anybody, kiddo," Lola explained. "They're just for dress up. They give people permission to be someone in the bedroom that they're not anywhere else. Think back to when you were a kid. Didn't you ever dress up?"

Sami nodded. "But I dressed up like a bride—in my mother's dress and veil."

"Okay, so you dressed for the wedding. These are for the honeymoon."

As time went on, the customers at Beneath the Sheets came to think of Sami as a confidante as well. After she'd been working there for a few weeks, they gradually began to include her in their conversations and even ask her advice. Not that Sami could offer much in the way of personal advice. Bruce hadn't been much of a teacher.

The customers didn't only ask for advice or a shoulder to cry on. They were also a pretty supportive bunch. And that came in handy the morning Sami noticed a little blurb in the Page Six column of the *New York Courier* that made her blood boil:

> It was a who's who in haute couture last night at the Ted Fromme Fashions bash to celebrate the design house's new line: Young and Powerful. The fashions, designed by up-and-coming soon-to-be-superstar Bruce Jamison, are targeted for young professionals. It's pretty much a given that Young and Powerful will be the hottest line from Fromme yet!

As she read the article, Sami could feel her face turn beet red. A blue vein popped out in her neck.

"Whoa, Sami, take a chill pill," Lola said, coming over to see what was wrong. "You'll have a stroke. What is it?"

Sami could only point to the news article.

"Son of a . . . ," Lola muttered as she read it. "He's still fakin' it."

Jenny, a quiet, mousy girl who was one of Lola's regular customers—and who surprisingly favored black leather bustiers—read the article over Lola's shoulder.

"This is the guy who used and abused our Sami," Lola explained to Jenny.

"Those are *my* designs," Sami wailed.

"Well, there's just one thing to do," Lola said.

"Exactly," Jenny agreed. "I'll make the voodoo doll."

Lola rolled her eyes. "I was thinking of something a little less physically painful."

"Oh," Jenny replied quietly.

"We've got to get this guy where it'll really hurt him—in his big fat male ego. We've got to make sure that you become more famous and successful than he'll ever be!"

"How do we do that?" Sami asked her.

"I don't know yet," Lola admitted. "But we'll find a way. I guarantee it, sugar-plum."

By six o'clock, Sami's anger had calmed. In its place was a feeling of utter defeat and pessimism. Bruce was a star, and she . . . well . . . the most Sami could say was that she probably created some of the most interesting bra displays in the Village. And to prove it, she placed a lavender padded B-cup on a mannequin.

"All right, that's it. Hold it right there!" a man's deep, obviously disguised voice came from behind.

Sami gasped and started to turn around.

"Don't move," the man warned.

Sami's heart was pounding. This was a robbery—or worse. Her father had been right: New York was a horrible place to live. She was going to die, here, in an *underwear* store. Her family would never live down the shame and—

"Oh man, we got her good!"

Sami recognized *that* voice immediately. "Rain!" she exclaimed with a mix of anger and relief. She turned around and faced Rain and Vin. It had been his voice she'd first heard.

"You should see your face!" Rain exploded into a fit of giggles that could be matched only by the hearty belly laughs coming from Vin.

"Classic," Lola guffawed from behind the counter. "You guys should consider a career in theater!"

"That was so *not* funny!" Sami barked at the three of them. "I thought you were criminals."

"We're here to commit a crime, all right," Vin informed her. "It's a kidnapping."

"What?"

"That's right," Rain agreed. "We're kidnapping you and forcing you to go out and forget your troubles."

"I don't feel like going out tonight—," Sami began.

"See, I told you that's what she'd say," Lola told Vin and Rain. "She's been in the dumps all day."

"You know what you need?" Rain told her. "Salsa."

"I'm not very hungry," Sami said, and sighed.

"Not the salsa you eat," Vin corrected her. "Salsa music. We're going dancing outside by the fountain at Lincoln Center."

"You're gonna love it," Rain added. "Live music, lots of people dancing. And best of all, it's free."

"I don't—"

"Sorry," Vin told her sternly. "You have no choice. We're the kidnappers. You have to do what we say." He took her by the hand and pulled her toward the door.

"Lola, didn't you want me to close up tonight?" Sami pleaded.

Lola shook her head. "Go have a good time. And that's an order."

By the time Sami, Rain, and Vin emerged from the number 1 train by Lincoln Center, the salsa band was in full swing. Men and women were dancing wildly on the platform surrounding the huge Lincoln Center fountain. They were hot and sweaty, but no one seemed to mind as they moved their bodies suggestively to the powerful Latin rhythm of the drums. "They sure didn't do dances like this at our school prom," Sami murmured.

"It's hot, huh?" Rain commented as she began to move to the beat.

Sami looked at her roommate with amazement. Rain had no inhibitions. Here she was, dancing, all by herself, in front of hundreds of strangers. It seemed as though everyone there noticed her— she was hard to miss, what with her wild red hair and long, lean body. But Rain didn't care if people stared. She just wanted to have a good time. Sami wished she could be more like that. But she knew that she would always be more of a behind-the-scenes type.

Sort of like Vin. Sami noticed that, like her, he was just standing there, watching. But, much to Sami's surprise, he wasn't looking at Rain. He was studying Sami's expression. She blushed slightly when she realized he'd been staring at her. "What're you smiling about?" she finally asked him.

"You," Vin said.

"Why?"

"You're funny," he told her. "So easy to

read. Like just then. You were wishing you could dance like Rain, but you'd never dare."

Sami blushed harder. He *did* know her well. But she wasn't going to let him know that. Playfully, she raised an eyebrow and tucked her tongue behind her cheek. "Oh yeah, well what am I thinking now?"

Vin laughed. "You're thinking I shouldn't be so sure of myself when it comes to you."

Sami sighed. He'd gotten her again.

"But don't worry, Sami," Vin continued. "When it comes to you, I never take anything for granted. You keep me on my toes . . . speaking of which, do you want to dance?"

"I've never done any dancing like this before."

"Well, you won't learn from me, I have two left feet," Vin admitted. "But I'm willing to give it a try if you are. Besides, no one will notice us. They're all too busy staring at Rain."

Sami laughed. That was true. Her roommate already had a circle of admirers. Tentatively she took Vin's hand, and together they tried to imitate the moves of the people around them.

Having Vin's strong arm around her waist made Sami feel more secure, and less conspicuous in her ill-fated attempts at salsa dancing. She figured no one would laugh at her when he was around. He'd never let that happen. Ever since she'd met him, Sami had always felt safe with Vin. He'd never do anything to hurt her. He was the kind of guy you might meet in Elk Lake: solid, honest, caring. If it weren't for that Brooklyn accent, he'd fit right in at home. Vin was a real friend, always in her corner.

"Okay, spin!" Vin interrupted her thoughts as he lifted his arm and twirled Sami around.

She laughed as she spun, feeling relaxed and joyous for the first time all day. The Latin beat and the company of her two best New York friends had been the perfect medicine to rid her of the lousy mood she'd been in since reading that article about Bruce. There were lots of good things in her life right now, she realized. It just took a night like this for her to remember.

Sami was so grateful to Vin that she reached over and gave him a small peck on the lips. His head shot back, surprised. But he didn't say anything. Instead, he smiled, lifted his arm, and twirled her around again.

Thirteen

"Listen, I gotta go down and convince some lawyers they don't want me on their jury," Lola told Sami early one morning as Sami arrived to help get Beneath the Sheets ready for customers. "You're in charge."

Sami gulped. She'd never been left alone in the store before. It seemed as if just as many of the customers came for Lola's advice as came to buy lingerie. She was certain they would turn and walk out the door the minute they realized Lola wasn't there. "But I don't know if I can—"

"Of course you can," Lola said, slipping her purple-and-blue poncho over her head. "And, anyway, I won't be gone long. Can you imagine me being chosen as a member of a jury of peers? Who could possibly be my peer?"

Sami laughed. "True. No one's like you, Lola."

"I'm definitely one of a kind," Lola agreed. "Okay, I'm off. I'll be back around five. Have fun, kiddo. Don't do anything I wouldn't do."

"That gives me plenty of room."

"You know it," Lola agreed.

After Lola left the shop, Sami busied herself putting together a fall display in the middle of the store. She'd considered doing a back-to-school display, but figured something seasonal was more appropriate for the age and interests of their average customer.

As Sami hung red, brown, and yellow lace panties on a fake tree, a woman walked into the shop. Sami recognized her right away. Nico was one of Lola's newer customers, and Sami liked Nico a lot. Nico was from a small town. She'd come to New York with her fiancé, Stan, who dreamed of making it as a video producer. At the moment, he was logging calls for MTV's *Total Request Live*. Nico was doing temp work—mostly typing and filing at big companies in Midtown.

"Hi, Nico," Sami greeted her. "What's doing?"

Nico looked around the shop. "You on your own today?"

Sami tried not to let her face fall as she sensed Nico's disappointment that Lola wasn't there. "Lola's on jury duty," she said. "But can I help?"

"I guess I'm looking for something really . . . daring."

"You *guess*?"

Nico blushed. "To tell you the truth, none of the nighties and panties and stuff have really been working. Stan's still preoccupied with not being able to do what he really wants to with work. I can't get him to notice me."

"That's tough." Sami studied Nico's face for a moment. "You seem kind of uncomfortable. Lola'll be back by five if you want to talk to her."

"No, it's not that," Nico admitted. "It's more that, well, I kind of feel weird wearing some of this stuff. But everyone says it's what men like, so . . ."

Sami shook her head. "Not all men like

this kind of stuff," she told Lola. "I don't think anyone in my hometown would go for it. They say they do, but . . ." Sami stopped herself as she realized that she could be killing a sale for Lola. "Anyway, you should wear what you feel comfortable in," she finished feebly.

"But I don't know what kind of lingerie would make me comfortable anymore. What do you sleep in?"

Sami thought of the big men's shirts she favored. *Nothing interesting there,* she thought. She looked around the room for inspiration. Her eyes fell on her bag, still on the counter. Her sketch pad was sticking out. A lightbulb went off in her head. "Nico, you know I'm a . . . I like to design, right?" she said.

"You're a good designer. Lola told me what happened at Ted Fromme."

Sami tried not to react as Nico opened that wound again. "Anyway, how about if I design a nightgown for you? Something that would make you happy."

"You would do that?" Nico asked.

Sami eyed Nico's height and build. "You're a size eight, right?"

Nico nodded.

"Okay. This won't take me too long. I'll have it for you on Wednesday."

Nico seemed a bit overwhelmed. "But what if—"

"No strings," Sami guaranteed. "It's like anything else here: If you don't want it, you don't have to buy it. But I think you're going to love it."

On Wednesday morning, Sami came to work with two nightgowns in hand. She was surprised to see Lola already there, shelving an order of gag boxers with lipstick kisses on them.

"Jury duty over already?" Sami asked. "I thought you'd be there for a week."

"Two days is all, if you don't get picked for a jury. Let's just say I wasn't the prosecution's dream juror. You know how we liberals can be."

Before Sami could answer, Nico entered the store. "So, are they ready?" she asked Sami anxiously.

"What's this about?" Lola asked as she walked over to Nico. "Don't tell me—you small-town girls are planning to take over the government. Can I help? I haven't been part of a coup in a long time."

Sami smiled. Lola certainly had some extreme ideas—not to mention an over-active imagination. "Nothing quite so political," she assured Lola.

"Sami just offered to make me some lingerie," Nico explained.

"Oh, she did?" Lola said in a tone that was only half teasing.

Sami was suddenly worried that Lola might not like her making things for the customers. "Well, Nico was telling me how she didn't feel comfortable in some of the skimpier stuff we sell, and I thought maybe her husband was picking up on her nervous-ness, and so he was tense, and maybe . . ." The words poured out of Sami's mouth.

But Lola wasn't at all upset. In fact, she was impressed. "Good thinkin'," she remarked. "He could be zeroing in on that uncomfortable vibe, and that's messin' with his personal rhythm, if you get my drift." Lola turned to Sami. "So, don't keep us waiting. Show us the rags."

"Yeah, the suspense is killing me," Nico agreed.

Sami lifted the first piece of lingerie from the bag. At first glance, it looked like a man's tailored shirt—complete with a pocket and a collar. But the material was distinctly feminine: white cotton, with small pale pink and blue flowers. Two darts sewn in the chest of the shirt ensured that Nico would look sexy and not at all masculine.

"I found this little fabric shop on Seventh Avenue," Sami told Nico. "They sell all sorts of great remnants."

"Oh, this is adorable!" Nico exclaimed, taking it from Sami. "I've got to try it on."

Sami watched as Nico went into the dressing room. She couldn't believe how nervous she felt. She really wanted Nico to like the nightgown. Not only would it make Nico happy—and Sami had really gotten to like the girl—but it would validate Sami's talents. The nightgowns were the first designs she'd finished and actually constructed since she'd left Ted Fromme Fashions. They meant a lot to her.

"So when did you manage to make that?" Lola asked nonchalantly.

"I've been sewing at night. It's a good thing Rain's not a light sleeper."

Lola laughed and busied herself folding panties. Sami was left to stand in the middle of the store and bite a ragged nail.

Finally Nico emerged from the dressing room. She was wearing the nightshirt and a pair of white socks. She slid across the floor with a huge smile on her face. "I feel just like Tom Cruise in *Risky Business,*" she exclaimed. "This shirt just makes me want to dance."

"You sure you're not thinking about *Dirty Dancing?*" Lola teased.

"I like that movie too," Nico replied. She turned to Sami. "You said you had two designs. What's the other one?"

"Well, this one's very different. I wasn't sure what you'd want, so I went in two separate directions." She pulled the second piece of lingerie from the bag. Then she handed Nico a short red-and-white gingham baby doll nightgown with lace sewn across the top.

"Oh, that's adorable!" Nico exclaimed. She reached out her hand and fingered the nightgown. "Is this flannel?"

Sami nodded. "It's going to get cold soon. Up where I'm from, people could never wear skimpy things. They'd freeze their tushes off!"

"I never thought of flannel as being sexy before," Nico said.

"It's not the clothes that are sexy," Sami said. "You're sexy if you feel good in the clothes. And this flannel is so soft. Besides, the lace adds the sex appeal."

Nico nodded. "I love the lace."

"It's sort of sweet and sexy all at the same time," Sami explained. "It's made for romance, not just lust."

"I *have* to try it on!" Nico squealed. She grabbed the nightgown and raced back into the dressing room.

"I never thought I'd see flannel in this store," Lola mused. "The times they are a changin'." She flashed Sami a smile to let her know she wasn't complaining.

It didn't take Nico very long to try on the new nightie. She emerged from the dressing room within a minute and twirled for Sami and Lola. "I feel so great in this. It's cozy and cute, but this lace . . ." She fingered the bodice. "I'll take them both," she told Sami. "How much?"

Sami didn't know what to say. "I . . .

um . . . I hadn't thought about that," she admitted.

Lola walked over and put her arm around Sami. "This is where I step in," she said. "Seeing as they were both custom made, I'd say they're worth sixty dollars apiece."

Apiece? Sami stared at her. She hoped Lola knew what she was doing. That seemed like a lot of money for two little nightgowns that Sami had whipped up in two days.

But Nico didn't seem to think so. "Okay," she agreed happily. "Let me just change and get my credit card."

After Nico had paid for the two nightgowns and left the store, Lola walked over to Sami and handed her three crisp twenty-dollar bills.

"What's this for?" Sami asked her.

"They're your design fee," Lola said simply. "You made the nightgowns, you deserve to be paid for them like any other professional."

Any other professional. Sami stared at the money in her hands in amazement. It was the first time she'd ever been paid for her design work. "I guess I'm a real designer now," she mumbled, dumbstruck.

"You always have been," Lola assured her. "You just had to believe it."

Sami squealed and threw her arms around Lola's neck. "Thank you!"

The next morning, two young women, probably in their early twenties, wandered into Beneath the Sheets. Sami could tell they were first timers. They kept lowering their heads, obviously trying not to stare at the more exotic items in the store, but unable to take their eyes from all the items on display.

Immediately, Lola went over and tried to put them at ease. "Can I help you?" she asked with her big, broad, welcoming smile.

"Are you Sami?" the smaller of the two women asked nervously.

Lola shook her head. "No, I'm Lola. That's Sami," she pointed behind the counter.

"Um, Nico sent us," the other woman told Lola. "She thought we might want to talk to Sami about some lingerie."

"Yes," her friend added. "We work at Casablanca Magazines, where Nico's been temping. She came in with these adorable nightgowns."

Lola turned and gave Sami a supportive grin. "Sami, these two clients are here for you. I think they might want to commission a few designs. Is that right, ladies?" she asked in a voice that was tinged with so much phony uptown professionalism that Sami had to choke back a laugh. But the two women seemed to be eating it up.

"That's exactly what we want," the tall woman agreed. "Nico told us you gave her the most beautiful demure lingerie." Her eyes went over toward a black see-through teddy hanging on the wall. "But I don't know if—"

"Oh, this is just our off-the-rack merchandise," Lola quickly assured her. "Sami's custom designs have a very different look and feel."

"Oh, of course," the tall woman replied.

"Sami, why don't you take these two clients into the office for a consultation?" Lola continued. "I can handle the traffic out here."

Still a bit bemused, Sami nodded and led the women back into Lola's office. On the way she grabbed a tape measure and a pad of plain paper and a pen. She wasn't quite sure what it was like to actually be a lingerie designer, but at the very least, she was determined to look the part.

Fourteen

Sami's career wasn't the only one on the upswing. Rain had spent the past few weeks focusing all her energy on getting ready for the Mollie Mack fashion show. The week had finally arrived. And now, Rain was backstage getting ready to go down a runway for the very first time, and Vin and Sami were there to witness the event.

"This is so exciting!" Sami whispered to Vin as they took their seats at the Mollie Mack fall fashion show. Rain had gotten them tickets for the event. It was Sami's first fashion show, and the excitement was almost overwhelming.

Vin, on the other hand, seemed decidedly nonplussed by the event. "I hope she doesn't trip or anything."

Sami looked at him, surprised. "Vin, how could you say that? Do you want to give Rain bad luck?"

Vin shook his head. "Sorry. It was just a joke. It's just that I'm sort of uncomfortable in this type of situation. Do I look like the kind of guy who's into fashion?"

Sami smiled. Despite the fact that Vin had tried to dress up for Rain's big night, he hadn't quite succeeded. His pants were just a little too tight, and his shirt had a tiny stain on the collar. At least his sport jacket, bought especially for the evening, fit him well, although the color made his skin look too olive.

"You just need the right girl to dress you," Sami suggested.

"That's just what I was thinking. . . ." He blinked suddenly as a photographer's flash went off right in his eyes. "What the—"

"I think he was taking a picture of Madonna. She's sitting right there, two rows ahead of us. Wow! Madonna! Can you believe it? She's gorgeous in person."

Vin shot Sami a playful glance. "She's not my type. I'm into someone—"

Sami grabbed his sleeve excitedly as an idea brewed in her mind. "Hey! You should ask Rain to fix you up with one of her friends from this show. I've met most of them. They're amazing!"

Vin's face fell. "That's not quite what I had in mind."

Before Sami could say another word, the music began. One by one the models came out, dressed in the hottest new Mollie Mack fall fashions. Camera flashes went off wildly as each girl took the stage, and video cameramen vied for the best spot to shoot the show. Fashion writers—all of whom seemed to be dressed in nearly identical chic black suits—scribbled notes frantically as the girls went by.

This year Mollie had gone with a total retro look—a throwback to her days on Carnaby Street. The music was all sixties and seventies period pieces as the girls strutted down the vividly painted multi-tiered catwalk, dressed in wetlook miniskirts, high go-go boots, and blouses in outrageous colors like electric orange and hot pink. The models were so heavily made up that Sami barely recognized Rain beneath the wild hair, dark black eyeliner, and huge false eyelashes. The fashion show was classic Mollie Mack, and by the sound of the appreciative murmur in the audience, it was another huge hit for the designer.

But Vin wasn't so sure that the clothes were anything great. In fact, as he and Sami left the show, he did nothing but complain. "Who could wear that stuff?" he asked. "Why doesn't she design things for real people?"

Sami couldn't argue. In a way, she'd been thinking the same thing. The Mollie Mack show was almost a costume performance— much like many of the other big designers' shows. It was as though their goal was to set a tone for the fashion industry, knowing full well that only jet-setters and celebs could ever really wear their overpriced, overdesigned clothing.

"And that *set,*" Vin continued as he and Sami headed outside to wait for Rain near the backstage exit. "What were they thinking? It was completely overdone. The designer and the carpenter should have gone with something much simpler. That way, the colors wouldn't have been competing with the clothes."

"Wow," Sami said. "I hadn't noticed that. You're right. My eye was going all over the place, but I couldn't figure out why."

"Sometimes it takes a carpenter to point things like that out," Vin told her. "It's just something you pick up over the years."

"You have an artist's eye," Sami told him.

"I *am* an artist," Vin said proudly. "My medium is wood. Sure, I install cabinets and wall moldings. But that's just my day job. The furniture I make, that's my art. Every piece I build is part of me."

Sami's mind thought back to the magnificent drafting table in her apartment. It was a piece of art. And a part of Vin. A true sign of friendship. She gave his hand a little squeeze.

Vin looked at her oddly, but didn't say anything.

"Look, there's Rain!" Sami shouted, letting go of Vin's hand to run over to her roommate, who was coming out of the models' dressing room and onto the sidewalk, where Vin and Sami were waiting for her.

"You were awesome!" Sami praised her as she ran over toward Rain.

"Do you really think so?" Rain asked hopefully.

Sami nodded. Rain's sudden insecurity surprised Sami. She always seemed so tough and assured. This small glimpse of a need for approval had popped up out of nowhere.

"What did you think?" Rain asked Vin.

"You didn't trip," Vin teased. "That was good."

"Thanks for the compliment." Rain laughed. "I did my best."

"In fact, you were the one good part of the show," Vin continued. "The only model with any character."

"You really stood out," Sami agreed.

"I was the only one with red hair. That helped," Rain explained.

"No, it was more than that," Sami said. "You were having fun up there, and it showed. When I'm a big designer, I'm only going to cast models who can have a good time on the runway." She started to laugh.

"What's so funny?" Rain asked her.

"The thought of me as a big designer," Sami said. "So far in my career as a professional designer, I've only sold six night-gowns."

"I don't think it's funny," Vin said.

"Me either," Rain seconded. "You gotta start somewhere. I have big dreams for us, Sam."

"For *us*?" Sami said.

"Oh, yeah," Rain grinned. "Since I'm the one who rescued you from the hellhole known as the Beresford Arms, I get first dibs on being the *face* of Sami Granger Designs."

"Speaking of faces . . . ," Vin said, laughing.

Sami joined in, giggling uncontrollably.

"What's so funny?" Rain demanded.

Vin pointed to the window glass in one of the neighboring stores. Rain glanced at her reflection. Her face was still made up heavily, with deep blush on her cheeks, liquid blue eyeshadow, white lipstick, and humongous black eyelashes that looked like spider's legs. While the effect was dramatic on stage, it was genuinely creepy close up.

"Ooo, I'm so Baby Jane." Rain grimaced.

"Do you want to clean up before we go out and celebrate?" Sami asked her.

Rain shook her head. "Let's go back to our neighborhood. I'll fit in just fine over there. Anything goes in the East Village, right?"

Lola was on the phone when Sami arrived at Beneath the Sheets early the next morning. Sami got to work immediately, going into the stockroom and pulling out a box of scented candles. She grabbed a ladder and began to arrange the candles on a high shelf behind the counter.

"Okay, thank you," Lola said, hanging up the phone. Then she looked up at Sami. "Oh no, you've got more important things to do today."

"But these just came in . . ."

Lola held up a stack of papers. "Do you know what these are?" she asked Sami.

Sami shook her head.

"They're orders for nightgowns, baby dolls, and nightshirts. And every one of these women wants *you* to design for her!"

Sami almost fell off the ladder.

"Whoa, be careful," Lola warned, helping her down. "I don't want to lose the girl who's putting this little love shack on the map."

"But there must be fifteen orders," Sami said, shocked as she flipped through the papers.

"Oh, no. Not that many. There's actually only fourteen. But some of them are for two or three items, so maybe it's more like twenty."

"But how . . ."

"Those two girls from Casablanca Magazines must have told their friends. And they told their friends. And so on . . . and so on," Lola said, imitating a classic shampoo commercial.

"But so many orders?" Sami said, sitting down, hard, on the floor. "There's tons to do here in the store all day. If I were going to make all these I'd have to work every night for a month, and even then I don't think . . ." Her stomach was turning over.

Lola shook her head. "I've got it all figured out. You're going to set up shop in the back office and design *full time*. I'll hire someone else to work out here. Maybe that kid Nico, the one who started you off. She's looking for something permanent, right?"

Sami jumped up. "Lola, you would really do that for me?" she asked.

Lola nodded. "Look, I'm a businesswoman, and your designs are going to bring in cash. But hell, I'd help you even if they wouldn't earn me a dime. Sami, you're one of the real ones. There aren't many of us left. We gotta stick together." She paused. "But there is one thing. . . ."

"Anything," Sami assured her.

"We gotta see a lawyer."

"Why?"

"I want to make sure we make everything official between us. If you're going to be a designer, you're going to have to make sure you get everything that's coming to you. You have to set up a business account at the bank, and have a lawyer who can handle setting up small businesses. I can't keep paying you commissions in twenty-dollar bills."

"But I trust you."

"I know you do. But you gotta think big. Bigger than this place. Sure, I'd love to have an exclusive deal with you, but that can't last forever."

Sami was confused. "What? What are you talking about?"

"You're destined for huge things, sugar pie," Lola said. "It's in your aura. And I just want to make sure that some nasty Bruce Jamison character can't come along and cheat you out of everything you deserve."

Sami could feel the tears building up in her eyes. This woman had no reason to take care of her. And yet that was exactly what she was doing. Taking care of her like a mother. Better than a mother, in fact, if Sami's own mother was the barometer of maternal instinct. Sami reached out and hugged Lola tight.

Lola let the girl cry for a moment, clearly unsure what this sudden surge of emotion was all about, but instinctively knowing that Sami had to let it out. Finally, she loosened Sami's grip, handed her a tissue, and gave her a smile. "Enough of this mush," she said. "Do you think the head of IBM sobs like a baby every time he gets an order for a computer? This is a *business*, right?"

Sami smiled. "Right."

"So you get in the back and start calling those women to make appointments for consultations and fittings. I'll call a lawyer friend of mine and get you an appointment."

"You know a lawyer?" Sami asked incredulously.

"What, you think the only people I know are the lovelorn and drag queens?" Lola asked. "I've got plenty of friends with desk jobs. I just don't like to admit it too often."

It was a few days later when Rain called Sami at work. "You're not going to believe who just called this house," Rain gushed excitedly into the phone.

"Ashton Kutcher?" Sami asked.

"I wish." Rain laughed.

"Brad Pitt?" Sami teased. "Justin Timberlake?"

"Now you're ruining the surprise."

"Why?" Sami asked. "Did Justin really call?"

"No. It's just that after those names, I guess Genevieve Bluster doesn't mean much."

Sami gasped. Genevieve Bluster was the editor of *Fashionista* magazine—the bible of the young fashion world.

"Genevieve Bluster called our apartment?" Sami asked incredulously. "Does she want you to do a cover?"

"She wasn't calling me. She was calling *you*. She wants to do a story—oh, I'm sorry, a *piece*—on you for their next issue." The last few words were practically screamed into the phone.

"It had to be a joke," Sami said, refusing to believe this was happening to her.

"No joke," Rain assured her. "I'd know that fake French accent anywhere. I've met her at about a thousand different parties from the agency."

"But—"

"No buts about it, Sam. I don't know why you're so surprised. *Fashionista* is part of the Casablanca Magazines publishing group. Your designs have been circulating around that place for days now."

It was true. Thanks to Nico's temping job, Sami had gotten a big in with a fashion magazine company. Sami made a mental note to do something incredibly nice for Lola's new shop girl.

"Oh, my God," Sami gasped as the realization began to set in. "What do I do now?"

"Well, for starters, call Genevieve back and tell her that tomorrow is just fine to meet with her reporter. Then meet me at home."

"Why?" Sami asked.

"Because we've got to work on your makeup, get your hair cut, and pick out a Sami Granger original for you to wear."

"I have to get all done up to meet a reporter?" Sami asked nervously.

"Genevieve is sending a photographer too. And not just any photographer. She's sending the hottest one around: *Franklin Beane*!"

After jumping around the store with Lola and Nico, Sami exhausted herself enough to make a relatively calm call to a woman who could literally make *or* break a designer's career. Fortunately, Genevieve was all *"oui"* and *"vous"* and running in a million directions. Sami spent more time on the phone with one of her assistants than confirming the appointment with the woman herself.

As soon as Sami hung up the phone with Genevieve Bluster, she made another call—to Elk Lake. Celia sounded weary as she answered the phone.

"Hey, Ceil, are you okay?" Sami asked.

"Sami. Long time no hear. How you been?"

Sami felt a twinge of guilt at that. It had been a while since she'd called Celia. "I'm sorry it's been so long," she said. "But things've been crazy here. I've been designing and sewing day and night."

"Sounds like things are picking up at Beneath the Sheets."

"Slowly," Sami told her. "People seem to really like the lingerie I'm designing. "

"Funny the places life takes you," Celia mused. "You never designed any lingerie before. It wasn't like you were the fashion queen of the slumber parties either. You always slept in your dad's old shirts. "

"I know. And now those shirts are the inspiration for a lot of my nightshirts," Sami explained. "And you're never going to believe this," Sami told her. "Tomorrow, I'm meeting with a reporter and photographer from *Fashionista* magazine! They want to do a piece on me. Me! Can you believe it?"

Sami had expected her best friend to be really excited. But, curiously, Celia was nonplussed. "Of course I believe it," Celia said. "You've always been great. Now other people are seeing it too. But Sami, a piece like that could get you a lot of work."

"I know, isn't that cool?"

"Well, that doesn't leave you much time for . . ."

"For what?" Sami asked.

"Well, for romance. I mean, you haven't had a date since that Bruce jerk," Celia said.

"Who needs romance? I'm going to be in *Fashionista*!"

Celia sighed. "It's wonderful, Sami, it really is. But don't you wish you had someone special to share it with?"

Now it was Sami's turn to sigh. Celia just wasn't getting it. "I *am* sharing it with someone. With you."

"That's not what I mean, and you know it," Celia said.

"Look, Celia, you live your life, and I live mine. I have different goals from yours."

"Do you think being a mother before I was twenty was in my game plan?" Celia blurted out.

Sami grew quiet. Celia had always been so supportive. And she seemed so happy with Al. It had never occurred to her that she might be jealous of Sami's life. Or maybe it was just those pregnancy hormones talking. Either way, Sami hadn't expected this response from her best friend. "Celia, I didn't mean to upset you. I just thought you'd be excited for me."

"You know, you only call when something exciting is happening to you," Celia replied tartly. "You don't call just to say hi, or ask how I am, or how your brother is. I'm not so sure your father wasn't right about you moving to New York."

That stung. Suddenly, Sami's guilt

about not calling was blanketed with a sheet of raw anger. "Well, it's not like you've been calling me either!" she spat out.

"I left you a message just last week. You never called me back."

Sami thought back for a minute. She vaguely remembered seeing a message from Celia. She'd meant to give her a call that night, but she'd had a client to meet with, and then she'd gone out for pierogis with Rain and Vin. After that, the message must've gotten buried.

"If you'd called, you would have known that I've been having more trouble with my blood pressure. It was pretty scary," Celia informed her curtly.

"Oh, Celia, I'm sorry," Sami replied earnestly. "I've been so selfish."

"Yeah, you have," Celia agreed.

"Are you okay?" Sami asked.

"I'm fine now. I can get out of bed in a few more days, now that my blood pressure's stabilized."

"That's good, at least."

"It is," Celia agreed. "And I'll tell you, Al's been so great about this. He's waiting on me like I'm a princess."

"I'm glad," Sami said. "And the baby?"

"She's fine," Celia told her.

"She?"

"See, you're not the only one with news. We saw her on the sonogram last week, and it's definitely a girl."

"Heaven help the girl who has my brother for a father."

Celia giggled. "I know. You and I are going to have to sedate him when she has her first date."

Sami laughed. "He'll be just like your dad. Remember the interrogation he used to give the guys who came to pick you up?"

Celia lowered her voice to sound like her father. "'And just what plans do you have for your life, young man?'" she said, imitating him. "And that was just the guys I dated in junior high!"

Before long, Celia and Sami were laughing and trading gossip again. Their disagreement had been brushed under the carpet. But Sami knew that didn't mean it had disappeared completely. Although she didn't want to admit it, the distance between them was growing wider.

Fifteen

Franklin Beane wasn't like any photographer Sami had ever encountered—not that Sami had had much contact with professional photographers. In fact, she'd only met two: the guy who had taken the photos at her senior prom, and the one who had taken the pictures at Al and Celia's wedding. And neither of those had ever leaped around the room like Franklin Beane did.

As Sami spoke to the reporter from *Fashionista* (Marla Simmons, a nervous girl who had starved herself way past fashionably thin), Franklin hopped up on counters, climbed ladders, and practically swung from the light fixture to take photos of Sami and her designs. From time to time he would run his fingers through his dark brown, shoulder-length hair and consider what part of his photography jungle gym he should climb up on next. But he wasn't at all intrusive, and after a while Sami barely remembered he was there. Franklin even managed to get a few photos of Lola, who was circling around Sami throughout the interview like a mama lioness protecting her young from a predator known as the media.

"So, what do the folks back home in the hinterland think of your success?" Marla asked Sami in a voice that was part Long Island, part fake British, and completely affected.

Sami bristled slightly at the reporter's dismissive tone. Lola noted her discomfort and before she could answer the question, the store owner butted in. "That would be *Elk Lake,*" she told Marla. "I know it's tough, being two whole syllables and all, but that's where Sami's from. And she's damned proud of it."

"Of course she is," Marla replied quickly, cowering into the high neck of her black leather jacket.

"My brother and sister-in-law are ecstatic!" Sami told her. "They helped me financially when I first arrived, and so they're sharing in all this."

"And your parents?" Marla asked.

"Well, my dad has had a hard time letting his little girl go off to New York by herself, but I think he'll come around," Sami said.

"What about your mom?"

Sami could feel the heat rising in her cheeks. "I'm not sure how she feels," she said simply, hoping Marla wouldn't read too much into her tone.

"Have you seen Sami's latest creation?" Lola interrupted, holding up a rich, full-skirted purple-and-gold nightgown with a laced bodice. "It's a variation on a medieval gown. Incredibly feminine era, the Middle Ages, doncha think?"

Sami glanced up gratefully in Lola's direction. Lola smiled back.

"Hey, Sami, why don't you try that one on?" Franklin asked her. "We can take a few shots of you in one of your designs."

"*Oh,* I'm not a model," Sami told him.

"Thank *God,*" Franklin replied. "The

last thing *Fashionista* needs is more models. I want you to show that your designs are for anybody, not just for models."

"In that case, why don't you ask Lola to put it on?" Marla suggested, obviously still smarting from Lola's Elk Lake comment.

"Oh, that's not my favorite design in the shop," Lola told her easily. "And I don't think you'd want to put the kinds of things I wear to bed in *Fashionista*." She pointed over to a display of extremely suggestive black leather panties and matching bras.

Marla blushed. Franklin laughed. "I'll bet you've been photographed plenty in your time," he teased Lola.

"Sure," she told him. "But those aren't for public viewing." She turned to Sami. "Go ahead, kiddo. You didn't let Rain put all that paint on your face for nothing."

Sami blushed. Rain *had* spent a long time making Sami up for this interview. Not only had she literally spent hours going through her makeup box, finding just the right shades for Sami's pale skin, she'd also arranged for one of her friends, an up-and-coming hairdresser named Snake, to cut Sami's long, straight locks into a shoulder-length bob that bounced up and down as she walked.

Now, as Sami headed into the dressing room at the back of the store and looked at herself in the mirror, she was amazed at the transformation. No one in the world would ever believe that she was from Elk Lake, Minnesota. She looked every bit like a sleek, sophisticated New York designer. She seemed comfortable in the look, unlike Marla, who seemed to be trying far too hard to be part of the fashion in-crowd.

Sami laced up the bodice of the nightgown and nervously fluffed her hair. She turned around quickly, making sure that there were no loose hems or open seams. She knew that there was a lot riding on this interview. If Marla and Franklin didn't like this design, it could mean the end of everything. *Fashionista* was the bible of the up-and-coming fashion world—a weekly introduction into what was sure to be the next new thing.

But as Sami emerged from the dressing room, she knew instinctively that, at least from Franklin's point of view, the design had worked its magic. She could see it in his deep-set chocolate brown eyes, which lit up as she entered the room. His face took on an excited hue, and he leaped up onto the cashier's counter, camera in hand. "Okay, Cinderella," he greeted her as he began snapping away. "Welcome to the fashion ball."

Lola and Marla stood off to the side as Franklin worked, urging Sami to swirl around, making her laugh and smile for the camera despite herself. All of her nervousness seemed to disappear in his enthusiastic presence. Only once did she blanch—at his suggestion that she give the camera her most sexy look. The thought of herself as some sex symbol was too funny for Sami even to imagine, and she burst into hysterics, which were dutifully recorded by Franklin's camera.

"Okay, that should do it," Franklin said finally. "Do you have everything you need, Marla?"

Marla nodded. "Got it. Should I wait for you?"

Franklin shook his head. "Nah. I've got to take these lights down and load them back into my van. Tell Gen I'll have these zapped onto her computer by the end of the day." Franklin held up his camera. "Digital cameras. You gotta love 'em."

Sami held out her hand to Marla. "Thank you so much for coming down here to see everything," she said sincerely.

"That's my job," Marla said. "It was nice meeting you, Sami."

Sami tried to study her face, searching for some clue as to how she had reacted to Sami's designs. But Marla's face was a blank slate, revealing nothing.

As Franklin packed up his lights, Sami went back into the dressing room and put on the black pants and magenta turtleneck Rain had picked out for her to wear that morning. She walked back into the main room of the store just as Franklin was preparing to return to the *Fashionista* offices. She walked over and reached out her hand. "Thank you," she told him. "It was fun."

"What, that's all I get?" Franklin asked her.

Sami was caught off balance. Just what was Franklin Beane expecting from her? Was she supposed to pay him for the photos? Sami wasn't experienced with the media, and she wasn't quite sure how this all worked. A wave of panic came over her. She could never afford to pay a famous photographer like him.

Franklin laughed at her reaction. "Well, Cinderella, even the prince got a glass slipper when the ball ended. I was hoping I could at least get your phone number."

Sami bit her lower lip. She'd sworn off men. She'd told that to Celia, Lola, Rain, Vin, and just about anyone else who would listen. Still, looking into Franklin's brown eyes, she softened slightly. He seemed so happy and full of life. He'd be fun to hang around with. This time, she'd just be smarter. "Okay," she said quietly, scribbling her home number on a piece of paper.

Franklin placed the paper in the inside pocket of his leather jacket and tapped it lightly. "I'll guard this with my life," he vowed. "Wouldn't want your number to get into the wrong hands."

"Who would that be?" Sami asked him.

"Anyone who could be considered my competition," Franklin said with a grin.

One week later, Sami sat behind the counter at Beneath the Sheets with her hands over her eyes. "I can't look," she told Nico and Lola. "What if it's awful?"

Lola picked up the latest issue of *Fashionista* and carefully scanned the pages until she came to the article she was searching for. "Here it is," she told Sami. "You want me to read it?"

"No. I mean yes. I mean . . . oh, I don't know!"

Nico peered over Lola's shoulder. "Ooo, Sami, you look gorgeous. Like a princess."

Still, Sami didn't uncover her eyes.

"I'm just going to read it," Lola said finally. "The headline reads, 'Dress Up on Halloween Night.'"

Sami gasped. "Oh, no! Marla thought my outfits were so awful, they looked like Halloween costumes?"

Lola kept reading:

"Sami Granger's new lingerie line is a real Halloween treat. Her long lines and soft fabrics will trick your honey into thinking he's seeing a lot more than is actually being revealed. She's managed to combine her northern Minnesota roots (she hails from a small, small, small town called Elk Lake) with an East Village sex appeal, obviously developed under the tutelage of Lola (no last name needed), owner of the downtown boutique Beneath the Sheets."

Lola stopped reading long enough to chuckle. "Whaddaya know? We're a boutique now."

"Keep reading," Nico urged her.

Sami was pretty sure she'd stopped breathing.

"Granger's collection is small, and her customer base is limited to just a few in-the-know customers. For the moment, Granger personally consults, designs, and sews the garments. But that won't last long. As soon as word gets out about Sami Granger's lingerie line, she'll have to expand into a full-fledged design business. This reporter only hopes that when that happens, the lingerie won't lose the warm personal touch the current line embodies."

Lola put the paper down on the counter. "Well, that sucks," she groaned.

Nico looked at her strangely. "Are you kidding? That was unbelievably great!"

Lola shook her head. "After people read that, we're going to be swamped by all those snooty Upper East Side trophy wives whose only job is to keep their hubbies hot. Not to mention trendy models, and, if I'm not mistaken, phony fashion writers like Marla Simmons." She sighed. "Ah, well. There goes the neighborhood."

Throughout this entire exchange, Sami sat speechless behind the counter. She'd gone from being a wronged receptionist, to being the subject of a positive—make that *really* positive—review in *Fashionista*. She sat back and let the realization of what had just happened sink in. But that moment of self-satisfaction didn't last long. The phone began to ring.

"I'll get it," Nico said, leaping up to answer the call. "Hello. How may I help you? Beneath the Sheets."

Lola rolled her eyes. "She's never going to get the hang of that."

Nico blushed, realizing what she'd just said. Then she returned to the caller. "Yes, she's here. One second, please." She held the phone out to Sami. "It's for you."

Sami took the phone, expecting to hear

the voice of one of her customers on the other end. Instead, a man's deep voice said, "Hello, Sami?"

"Yes?" Sami said, not recognizing the voice.

"What, have you forgotten all the little people already?"

"Vin!" Sami exclaimed. "You don't sound like you."

"I just woke up," Vin replied. "This is how I sound when I haven't spoken in eight hours. But Rain just pushed a copy of *Fashionista* under the door. I wanted to congratulate you. We need to celebrate tonight."

"Sure . . . I . . ." Just then, there was a beep on the phone. "Hold on, Vin, that's the call-waiting." She pressed the button on the receiver. "Hello?"

"Cinderella! Howyadoin'?" Franklin Beane's unmistakable voice rang out from the other end.

"Amazing," Sami told him. "Thanks to you . . . and Marla. The article was great. And your pictures . . . I've never seen anything like them."

"Aw shucks, ma'am, t'weren't nothin',"

Franklin laughed, taking on an old-time Western voice.

"Yes, they were! They were incredible. I don't know how to thank you."

"I've got an idea," Franklin replied, his voice taking on a slightly more seductive tone.

"Franklin, I . . . I hardly know you," Sami stammered.

"True. But when you get to know me, you'll adore me." His voice grew more playful and far less intimidating.

"No doubt." Sami laughed.

"So how about getting to know me tonight? I have to photograph the Giovanni evening wear show, and then there's a dinner party at Le Cirque."

"Le Cirque?" Sami gasped. "I've always dreamed of going there!"

"Great. Meet me at the Giovanni showroom at seven. I have to take some preliminary shots there, and then we'll head over to the show."

"Okay," Sami said slowly.

"Talk to you later," Franklin said, hanging up the phone.

"You're going to Le Cirque?" Nico

asked as Sami stood there, holding the phone in her hand.

Sami nodded. "Franklin Beane asked me to go to the Giovanni party."

"Wow!" Nico exclaimed.

"Excuse me," Lola interrupted. "But don't you have someone else on the other line?"

"Oh, Vin!" Sami exclaimed, quickly pushing the call-waiting button to bring Vin back onto the phone. "Sorry about that," she said quickly.

"No problem," Vin assured her. "I had time to build a table."

"Very funny," Sami joked.

"I hear girls love a guy with a sense of humor," Vin told her. "So about celebrating. I was thinking about maybe going over to SoHo Bar and Grill for a drink and then over to Gold Star Sushi—"

"It sounds great," Sami said. "But can we do it tomorrow night? Franklin Beane just invited me to the Giovanni show and the party afterward."

"Sure." Vin's voice was quiet and disappointed.

"I have to go with him tonight," Sami

insisted, trying not to hurt her buddy's feelings. "I mean, I owe everything to him."

"You don't owe anybody anything," Vin told her loyally. "Your talent is what's going to make you a success."

"But those pictures—"

"They were nice. You look better in person." He took a deep breath. "Okay. Tomorrow, then."

"Maybe we could ask Rain to come along. You know, the Three Musketeers out on the town?" Sami suggested cheerfully.

"Sure," Vin said evenly. "Whatever you want."

Sixteen

The next few weeks were a whirlwind. Sami wished she could savor each moment, but she was so busy that she couldn't take the time to commit all the excitement to memory. She spent all day designing and making lingerie for her ever-expanding client base. Her nights were spent with Franklin, attending fashion parties and high-profile charity events. Once or twice she'd even seen Ted Fromme at a few of the events. And although her former employer had tried to make eye contact with her, Sami had managed to blow him off completely—which brought her far too much joy.

It seemed to Sami that Franklin knew everyone who was anyone in the New York fashion world. Glamorous models flocked to him wherever he went, drawn to him like elegant moths dancing around a flame. But Franklin barely paid them any notice. When Sami was on his arm, he had eyes for no one else.

On the other hand, Sami didn't feel as though she knew him any better now than when she'd first met him. She and Franklin had barely had any time alone together, other than in cabs as they darted from one event to another. Franklin never had time for a quiet private dinner, or a Saturday afternoon in the park. He was always working, or heading off to another industry party. In fact, although they'd been dating for several weeks now, he and Sami hadn't shared more than a quick good night kiss from time to time. Anytime Sami had suggested he stop up at the apartment for a drink, or just to talk, he'd begged off, explaining that he had an early meeting or photo shoot to get to.

Which didn't mean that Franklin didn't show his affection in other ways. He was charming, funny, and obviously smitten with her. Unlike Bruce, he seemed to be genuinely impressed with her talent, and he showed his support in the most amazing ways. One of the tokens of his affection was delivered to Beneath the Sheets one morning in mid November.

"What's that?" Lola asked when a box appeared in the doorway.

"It's for Sami," Nico said as she signed for the delivery. "It's from Franklin."

Lola looked at the package. "Can't he just send roses like anyone else?" She turned toward the back office. "Sami," she called out. "Frankie's sent over another overpriced gift, I think."

Sami walked out of the office. "You know he hates being called Frankie," she scolded Lola.

Lola shrugged.

"I wonder what it is," Sami mused as she began to unwrap the sleek black packaging.

"Come on," Nico urged her. "Speed it up. The curiosity is killing me." She reached over and began to rip at the paper.

"Wow, it's from La Parisienne," Nico

said, sounding impressed that Franklin would send something from what was quite possibly the most expensive boutique on Madison Avenue.

Sami gingerly opened the lid of the box. Inside was a pale blue multitiered dress. "Wear this tonight. Will pick you up at 8:00 for an adventure."

"Oooo, that's so romantic," Nico cooed.

"What makes him so sure you're free?" Lola wondered disparagingly. "Does he think you're just waiting around for his call?"

Sami picked up the dress and held it in front of her. It was the color of her eyes. "Don't you love this dress?" She sighed.

Lola shook her head. "I think you've designed nicer stuff," she told Sami. "And don't you have a deadline on that bridal trousseau?"

"Ooo, I almost forgot," Sami admitted, racing for the office.

"I'll hang up the dress so it won't crease." Nico reached beneath the counter for a plastic hanger.

"Thanks," Sami called back.

As Sami left the room, Nico looked

curiously at Lola. "You don't like Franklin very much, do you?"

Lola shook her head. "I've seen his type before. He treats women like ice-cream cones. Sami's the flavor of the month right now. Before long, he'll switch tastes and put some other scoop on his cone."

"I don't know. He seems to really like her. I think maybe Sami's met her soul mate," Nico said.

"I agree," Lola replied.

Nico looked surprised. "But you said—"

"She's met him, all right," Lola finished her thought. "She just doesn't know it yet."

There wasn't time for Sami to go home and dress after work, so she got ready for her big adventure in the dressing room at Beneath the Sheets. The shop closed at 7:30, which left Sami little time to get out of her work clothes and into the elegant evening dress Franklin had sent over.

As she went into the poorly lit bathroom to put on her makeup, she could hear Lola moving tables around in the front room. Then she heard voices as people entered the store. By the time Sami walked out into the front room, a full-fledged poker game was under way.

"Hey, Sami," Jenny, the mousy regular customer with a fetish for leather, called from behind a pile of chips.

"Don't you look adorable," commented Madame Lexis, a six-foot drag queen in gold lamé. "But you might want to do up your eyes a little more. I have some false eyelashes in my purse if you . . ."

Sami shook her head. "No, that's okay. I don't know where I'm going, so I don't want to go too heavy on the makeup."

"Ooo, a surprise!" KC, one of Lola's friends from her more Bohemian days, cooed. "I just love surprises. Lola, do you remember that time you and I popped out of that cake at Bobby Dylan's birthday party? I tell ya, that boy almost swallowed his harmonica. Do you know who Bob Dylan is, Sami?"

Sami nodded. "He's pretty famous where I come from. He was from Minnesota too. Hibbing, I think."

"Yeah, even if he wouldn't have admitted it in those days. He wanted everyone to think he was a drifter, like Woody Guthrie or something," KC recalled.

"Enough with the music history lesson," Lola barked, taking time to slip a cigar between her lips. "Whaddaya bid?"

Sami looked at her, surprised. "Lola, I didn't think you smoked anymore."

Lola shook her head. "I don't. I quit centuries ago. This is all for effect. It's not even lit."

Just then, the bells above the door rang out. Sami's heart skipped a beat as the door opened. Her adventure was about to begin.

"Oh, wow!" Franklin said as he walked in the shop. "You look stunning."

Madame Lexis stood up and curtsied. "Thank you. You look nice too."

Franklin wasn't at all flustered by Madame Lexis. After being a photographer in the fashion business for several years, nothing could totally surprise him. "Thank you," he replied. Then he turned his attention to Sami. "I knew that dress would be perfect. Give us a spin, love."

Sami dutifully spun around, and the multitiered skirt flew up around her like a ballerina's tutu.

"Careful you don't get dizzy," Jenny warned. "You wouldn't want to get sick."

"Why not?" Lola murmured under her breath. "I am."

If Franklin heard Lola, he didn't mention it. Instead, he gestured toward the door. "Your chariot awaits."

"Where are we going?" Sami asked, as excited as a kid at Christmas.

"It's a surprise," Franklin teased.

"Oh, please tell me," Sami pleaded, hugging him tightly and kissing him squarely on the lips.

Franklin laughed. "All right, I surrender. I can't resist you when you get like that. We're going to the Year in Fashion Awards."

Sami stared at him. "No way."

"*Way.*"

"Brilliant conversationalists, aren't they?" Lola remarked sarcastically. She tossed three red chips onto the pile in the center of the table.

Sami frowned at her, but took the teasing good-naturedly. "It was impossible to get tickets for that show."

"Nothing's impossible, Sami," Franklin said. "Stick with me, kid. You'll see things you've never dreamed of."

⭐

Sami had never actually walked down a red carpet before—at least not in real life. In her dreams, she'd done it a million times. But this was no dream. Like all the invited guests, Sami and Franklin were taking their turn strolling along the red path to the theater. As they made their way past the crowds of adoring fans and assembled photographers, Sami recognized a few people on the carpet nearby. There was Stella McCartney, accompanied by her famous father, Paul. Sami wished her dad could see her standing not more than twenty feet from a former Beatle. She winced a little, realizing that she couldn't even call him to tell him—they hadn't spoken a word since that morning four months ago, when Sami had gotten on the bus and gone to New York without his blessing. Not that Sami hadn't thought about calling her dad. It's just that every time she picked up the phone, her heart raced so fast that she'd hung up in a panic before she could dial the number.

She quickly struggled to shake all thoughts of Elk Lake from her mind.

Minnesota was thousands of miles away from this place. This was a New York experience. The kind of thing that could only happen in the Big Apple.

"Cindy, darling, how are the kids?" Franklin asked, pulling Sami over toward Cindy Crawford.

"Franklin," Cindy replied. "Nice to see you. We're all well."

The cameras flashed in Cindy Crawford's direction, and she turned slightly to give the photographers a better look at her dress.

Rebecca Romijn-Stamos passed by next, waving to the crowd and then posing for the cameras. Franklin, pulling Sami along behind him, stopped for a moment to greet Ralph Lauren, who was speaking to a television reporter. Coming up next, Sami recognized Mollie Mack, who was scheduled to receive a lifetime achievement award.

As Sami passed by Mollie Mack, she heard someone call out her name. "Sami, Sami Granger," a man's voice, lightly tinged with a Southern accent, called out. Sami turned around and came face-to-face with Ted Fromme.

She wanted to turn away, but there was nowhere to go. She couldn't avoid Ted here. There were lights flashing everywhere and people all around. She looked for Franklin to give her support, but he was busy chatting up a group of models who were standing beside Iman and her husband, David Bowie.

"Congratulations on your success," Ted said slowly.

"Thank you."

"Everyone's talking about you," Ted continued. "You're a rising star."

"Just like Bruce Jamison," Sami replied with a touch of venom in her voice.

"Yes, well, that didn't quite work out as I'd hoped," Ted replied, sounding embarrassed. "He hasn't been able to come up with anything as potent as his first line."

"Maybe that's because his first line wasn't *his* at all," Sami snapped.

Before Ted could answer, Franklin took Sami by the arm. "We've got to get inside," he whispered to her.

As they walked off together, Franklin looked curiously at her. "What were you talking to Ted Fromme for? He's yesterday's news."

Sami smiled. "You're right," she said. "Heck, I've already forgotten him."

Sami didn't wake until late the next morning. She and Franklin had been to the show's after-party, and since Beneath the Sheets was closed on Sundays, she'd opted to take advantage of the extra time for some well-needed shut-eye.

When she finally ventured out into the living room, she found Rain and Vin happily ensconced on the couch, giggling over something in the newspaper.

"Reading the comics?" she asked them.

"Sort of," Rain replied between giggles. "I mean, it's got pictures and it's humorous, but . . ."

"Let's just say it's not *Classic Peanuts,*" Vin finished her thought.

"So what's so funny?" Sami asked.

Rain went to hand the paper to Sami, but Vin reached out his arm to stop her. "I don't think it's something she'd laugh at," he suggested to Rain.

"I don't know about that. Sami's got a good sense of humor. She's dating a clown, remember?" Rain giggled.

Sami reached over the couch and grabbed the paper out of Rain's hands. She looked down at the page. "You were laughing at Page Six?" she said, referring to the notorious gossip column in the paper. Then she took a closer look. The page was filled with behind-the-scenes pics of the previous night's Year in Fashion Awards. There were shots of Cindy Crawford, Mollie Mack, Dick Clark, David Bowie, and Iman. "What's so funny about these?" she asked curiously.

"Look closely," Rain said. "What do all those photos have in common?"

Sami looked at the page, scanning the pictures for one common thread. And then she found it: Franklin was in every one of the shots. He wasn't the center of attention, of course, but his name was mentioned in each caption.

"He sure gets around," Vin said as the look of comprehension formed on Sami's brow.

"For a photographer he certainly makes it his business to wind up on the other end of the lens whenever possible," Rain added.

"Can he help it if he has a lot of friends

in the business?" Sami asked defensively.

"Oh, yeah. I'm sure Dick Clark is a close, personal friend of Franklin Beane's," Rain countered, pointing to a photo of the seventy-something-year-old entertainment icon who'd produced the show. Franklin was standing just slightly to his right in the picture. Dick Clark didn't appear to notice him at all.

Sami scowled and poured herself a cup of coffee. "You didn't seem so cynical when Franklin offered to take some head shots of you for your portfolio."

"I didn't say he wasn't a great photographer. I'm just saying he's also an opportunist," Rain replied.

Sami sat down at the table and looked over the page again. Suddenly, her eye fell on a box at the bottom of the page. It was a blind item—a piece of gossip that didn't use names but somehow let everyone know exactly who the reporters were talking about.

What hotter-than-hot fashion photog was caught snugglin' and sizzlin' with downtown's reigning princess of lingerie at a dark corner table during the Fashion Awards after-party? We were just wondering, does she wear her own pj's to bed?

Sami blushed as she read the item. "That's not fair!" she moaned. "Franklin just gave me a peck on the cheek at the party. They made it seem as though we were making out or something. And I slept right here, in my own bed . . . alone."

Vin shrugged.

"Really," Sami assured him.

"Oh, I believe you," Vin said. "But the press writes what people want to believe, not necessarily what's true."

"At least they didn't use my name," Sami said.

"You're right," Rain said. "No one would ever guess that Franklin was the hot-ter-than-hot photographer, and you were downtown's reigning princess of lingerie." She bowed down low. "Your Majesty," she said with an exaggerated British accent before exploding into giggles once again.

Sami threw the paper at her. Rain ducked just in time to miss being decapitated by the oncoming gossip page.

"I'm just glad my dad doesn't read the *Courier*," Sami said. "He'd be on the next plane to drag me back to Elk Lake."

Just then, the phone rang. Rain picked up the receiver. "Hello?" she said. "Just a second. I'll get her."

"Is it for me?" Sami asked.

Rain nodded. "Speaking of Elk Lake . . . ," she said mysteriously.

"Oh, no. It's my dad?" Sami asked.

"Relax." Rain winked. "It's Celia."

Sami breathed a sigh of relief and took the phone from Rain. "Hey, Celia. How are you feeling?" Sami asked as she headed toward the bedroom and shut the door. Ever since Celia had chastised her about being self-centered, Sami had started each of their conversations by focusing on Celia's health and news from home.

"I'm great. Fit as a fiddle. The blood pressure's under control, and I've been taking walks more often. It's fun to get out. Not as fun as the outings you've been having, but—"

Sami gasped. Had the *Courier* reached Elk Lake? "What do you mean?"

"I was watching E! this morning and I saw a clip of Ralph Lauren being interviewed at some big awards show. Guess who I saw beside him?"

"Who?"

"You, silly. And a long-haired hottie who I can only imagine was that Franklin Beane fellow you've told me so much about."

Sami thought back to the night before. She vaguely recalled Franklin cozying up to Ralph Lauren while he was talking to a reporter, but she hadn't realized either of them had gotten in the shot. "We were there," Sami told her. "I didn't know we were on TV, though."

"You were," Celia said. "And that's not the coolest part."

"It's not?"

"No. The coolest part was that Mac saw you. He called right after it aired. Apparently the TV in the coffee shop was tuned to E! during the breakfast rush."

Sami sighed. "How'd he take it?" she asked nervously.

"Well, he was kind of shocked at your short hair and all that makeup you were wearing." Celia laughed. "But he acted like the ultimate proud papa. Made everyone think it was his idea that you move to New York."

"Slightly revisionist history," Sami murmured bitterly.

"I'll say. And everyone in the place knew it too. But apparently Mac just kept going on and on about how you were this hot new designer and everyone wanted to wear your stuff."

"How'd he know that?" Sami asked.

"Al and I've kept him up to date. Of course he never once mentioned that you design lingerie—or, 'unmentionables,' as he likes to call them."

Sami laughed. Her lingerie was nothing compared with some of the other items in Beneath the Sheets. Now *those* were "unmentionables"!

"Anyhow, some of the people in the coffee shop started ribbing Mac about how he'd tried to keep you at home and how he hadn't even seen you since you moved in July, and the next thing anyone knew, he was on the phone ordering three plane tickets to New York City."

Sami gulped. *"Excuse me?"*

Celia laughed. "You heard me. We're all coming to visit you—we'll be in on Thursday!"

"What Thursday?"

"This Thursday!" Celia said. "Good thing, too, because another few weeks and I won't be able to fly anymore."

"But—but, Dad . . . in New York?"

"I know, it sounded weird to me, too. But I think the one thing he fears more than New York is losing face with his friends back here. If he didn't go, they'd rib him forever," Celia said.

"Thursday?" Sami repeated. "It's so . . . so soon. And I don't even know where I'd put all of you. This apartment is so small, and it's a walk-up, which you can't do because you'd never be able to get up the stairs. And Franklin and I have a big benefit to go to on Thursday. He's already gotten the tickets and I can't—"

"That's okay," Celia said, her voice suddenly losing some of its enthusiasm. "We can see you on Friday. Just make us a reservation at some hotel. And don't worry, we'll only stay a week."

"Come on, Celia, don't be like that," Sami pleaded. "I want to see you, you know that. It's just that life here is so busy. But I'll clear Friday and most of the weekend, I promise."

Sami spoke to Celia for a few more moments before hanging up. "Oh, this is just awful," she moaned as she walked back into the living room.

"What's the matter?" Rain asked, concerned at the look of utter panic in Sami's face. "Is Celia okay? Is it the baby?"

"Oh, no," Sami assured her. "She's fine. They both are. It's just that she, Al, and my dad all saw me on TV."

"You were on TV?" Rain asked.

"Standing with Franklin behind Ralph Lauren while Ralph was being interviewed."

Rain began to laugh. "I'll say this for Franklin: He knows how to be in the right place at the right time."

"Come on, this is serious," Sami said. "Suddenly Dad's acting all proud and everything. He's coming to New York, with Celia and Al, on Thursday!"

Vin looked at her curiously. "But that's a good thing, right?"

"Wrong."

"Wrong?" Vin said. "I thought you wanted to patch things up with him."

"Over the phone," Sami told him. "Not here. Can you imagine my dad in New York? I can just see him in his big snorkle parka and boots wandering around the Village—"

"So what?" Rain interrupted. "It's not like he'd be the weirdest-looking guy in this neighborhood."

"And he's going to want to meet Franklin. I can only imagine what *he'll* think of my dad—or of Celia and Al, for that matter."

"What's wrong with them?" Rain asked. "It's not like they're the Beverly Hillbillies, you know. She's your best friend—other than me, of course. And he's your brother."

"They're also the ones who helped you move here in the first place," Vin chimed in.

"I know," Sami agreed. "But they're

just so different from the people I know here."

"They don't sound all that different," Vin said.

Sami didn't look so sure. "Franklin and my family. Oh, that'll be just great. What's he going to do when they start discussing hunting or ice fishing?"

Vin shook his head as he stood up from the couch. He turned to Rain. "I've got some work to do. Call me later if you want to catch a movie."

"What's with him?" Sami asked Rain as the door closed behind Vin.

Rain shrugged and grabbed her jacket from the coat rack. "I'm going out for a run," she said. "You might want to call and make reservations at the Fifth Avenue Hotel. It's in a much more chic area of the Village."

"Is it expensive?" Sami asked.

Rain shrugged. "Everything comes with a price, babe," she said as she headed out the door.

Seventeen

After much coaxing from Lola, Rain, and Vin, Sami decided to take Thursday afternoon off to meet her family at the airport before heading to the benefit at the Metropolitan Museum of Art. Vin had cleared his afternoon calendar and volunteered to drive her out to JFK Airport in his van. He knew this was one errand Sami didn't want to go on alone.

As she and Vin drove to the airport, Sami became more and more nervous. She knew that the purpose of Mac's visit was more than he'd led Celia to believe. Mac had taken ribbing from his friends before and it had never made him leave Elk Lake.

Not even when his wife had left him. He was going to try to convince her to come back to Elk Lake—of that, Sami was certain. She was less certain, however, that she'd be able to withstand another barrage of attacks from him. Or worse yet, a Mac Granger guilt trip. Sami's dad was the king of guilt. Either way, he would be hard to deal with face-to-face. That's why she'd left for New York before he'd ever woken up. It hadn't been mature, but she and Celia had both decided that it was the way it had to be.

Sami had hoped to get to JFK Airport early, but she and Vin hit a patch of traffic because of some of the never-ending construction that plagued New York City's roadways. So by the time the van pulled up in front of the terminal, Al, Celia, and her father were already waiting in the taxi line.

"There they are," Sami said nervously. But she made no move to get out of the van.

"Where?" Vin asked.

Sami sighed. "I'm sure you can pick them out."

"It's not like they're wearing a sign that

says, 'Look at us, we're tourists from a small town.'"

Sami laughed for the first time since she'd gotten in the van. "Just look for the group that includes a very pregnant woman, her husband, and a very angry man in a huge down jacket."

Vin laughed and looked around. Sure enough, there they were, exactly as Sami had just described them. "Oh, there they are. They've only got one or two more people and then they're next in line. Do you want to get out and go over to them, or should we just wait for them to get into a taxi and tail them all the way back to Manhattan?"

"Is this a multiple-choice question?" Sami asked hopefully.

Vin gave her a playful shove. "Get out of the van."

"Come with me?"

Vin shook his head. I can't just leave the van here: They'll tow me. But I promise to dial 911 the minute your father turns into a werewolf. I think there's a full moon tonight."

"Not funny." Sami grimaced as she

unhooked her belt and got out of the van. She walked slowly toward the taxi line, feeling more like someone heading to the gallows than a girl who was about to see her family for the first time in four months. Of course, in Sami's mind, it was all sort of the same thing.

Celia was the first one to recognize Sami. "There she is!" she shouted, leaving Al and Mac Granger behind as she waddled over toward Sami.

"Wait for us," Al called out, grabbing their bags and following his wife. Sami's dad didn't hurry, however. Instead, he walked cautiously, eyeing his daughter suspiciously, trying to determine whether she was in a fighting mood.

Sami wasn't looking at her dad, though. She was too busy hugging Al and patting Celia's belly.

Sami was amazed at the transformation that had taken place in her brother. Al looked at Celia with a sense of devotion and caring that Sami had never seen on his face before. He stood tall and proud as Sami patted Celia's stomach and cooed over her pregnant glow.

Celia had changed as well. Her usually chiseled features were camouflaged by a growing roundness in her face. And her stomach looked huge—as though she'd swallowed a watermelon that had begun to spread around her hips. Not even the plaid wool maternity cape she was wearing could hide the fact that Celia had taken advantage of her pregnancy to eat whatever she chose. But like Al, she also seemed more mature and settled. The wild schoolgirl who would try anything at least once had been replaced by a mother-to-be. Sure, Celia still had the same lilting laugh, but her smile had something wise and knowing behind it. It was as though Celia had learned a secret that Sami didn't yet know.

But Celia wasn't the one who'd changed the most. That award went to Mac Granger. Sami was shocked at just how much older her dad seemed. In Elk Lake he'd seemed so tall and strong. But here, in New York, surrounded by people of all sizes, shapes, races, and religions, he seemed small and meek. His back was obviously bothering him. He was stooped slightly and kept shifting his weight from foot to foot. One look at his nervous face and it was obvious that he was overwhelmed by the crowded city airport.

Suddenly all of Sami's fears washed away. There was nothing this man could say or do that would make her go back home against her will. He wasn't frightening at all. They were on her turf now. No matter what games her father might try to play, Sami had the home court advantage.

"Hi, Dad," she said in a strong, confident tone. "Welcome to New York."

Mac shook his head. "Some welcome. You should have seen the lines waiting to get the luggage. And now this taxi line. Instead of the Big Apple, they oughtta call this place the Big Line."

Celia sighed. "You haven't seen Sami in four months, and that's all you can say? Look at her. She's so sophisticated and hip."

"I liked her better the way she used to look. What made you cut your hair, anyway?" Mac groused. "And what's with all that makeup? You could work in a bordello. Oh yeah, I forgot, isn't that sort of what you're doin'?"

Sami shook her head. "I design *lingerie,* Dad."

"Well, where else do people wear that stuff?" Mac shot back.

Al stepped between his sister and his father. "I think you look great, kiddo," he said. "Success has been good for you."

"Well, I don't know how successful I am," Sami said. She turned to Celia. "I still haven't put Elk Lake on the map."

"You will," Celia assured her. "Now, did you drive here? Or are you taking a taxi back with us? I've got to get off my feet."

"My friend Vin volunteered to drive. His van's over there."

As they walked to the van, Sami was pointedly aware that her father had made no attempt to hug her, or even greet her. But then again, she hadn't, either. It seemed to her that she and her father had more in common than either one of them would ever admit.

During the ride back to Manhattan, Vin kept the conversation light and far from anything that could get Sami into any trouble with her dad. He pointed out various landmarks and talked about New York history with the confidence and knowledge of a professional tour guide. Celia and Al laughed at his jokes, and even Mac seemed interested by Vin's tales of the city.

"You know, for a New York boy, you're all right," Mac admitted as Vin pulled the van up in front of the Fifth Avenue Hotel. "If it weren't for that Brooklyn accent, you could be right out of Elk Lake."

"Thank you, sir," Vin said as he hopped out of the van to help Al with the bags.

Sami got out as well. "Look, tomorrow we'll spend the whole day together. I know this great Italian restaurant where the waiters sing opera."

Mac rolled his eyes.

"Oh, I think you'll like it, sir," Vin said. "The meatballs are huge."

"If you say so," Mac replied, unsure.

"Besides, tonight we're all going to that steak house, remember?" Vin said. Sami smiled at him, grateful that on the way into town he'd volunteered to show her family a great local place for dinner that night.

"How could I forget a big, juicy steak?" Mac asked.

"I wish I could come, but this benefit is very important. It's for the costume collection at the museum," Sami apologized for about the billionth time.

"It's okay, Sam," Celia assured her. "Just make sure you stop by the hotel before you leave. I want to see your dress—and that very large male accessory you'll have on your arm." Her eyes grew playful, and for a moment Sami caught a glimpse of the best friend she remembered.

"I promise," Sami said. "We'll be there at seven."

Al put his arm around Celia. "We'd better get settled in our room, sweetheart. You need to take a nap. Remember what the doctor said."

"What?" Sami asked anxiously. "What did he say?"

"Nothing," Celia assured her. "I'm just supposed to rest. I'm seven months pregnant, remember? I'm getting to the end of this thing, so naturally I'm a little tired."

Sami smiled. "I can't believe she's almost here!"

Al laughed. "Auntie Sami."

Sami wrinkled her nose. "That sounds awfully weird."

"If you think that's weird, try getting used to being called Mommy," Celia replied.

"Don't give her any ideas," Mac interrupted. "Who knows what kinds of people she meets at that store she works in."

"On that note," Al said, pushing his father toward the hotel lobby, "we'll see you later, Sami. And we'll meet you at that restaurant around eight o'clock, Vin."

"Just give the cab driver the address on that slip of paper," Vin told him. "He'll take you right to the door."

As Sami and Vin got back in the van, Sami breathed a huge sigh of relief. "Well, that's over," she said. "It was nice of you to volunteer to have dinner with them tonight. You didn't have to do that."

"I like them. They're a lot like my family—only with accents."

Sami laughed. "Excuse me?" she asked him. "Mr. Brooklynese himself thinks *my* family speaks with an accent? How youse guys doin', anyways?" she teased in an exaggerated Brooklyn accent.

"Point well taken," Vin agreed. "Anyhow, I like them."

"They like you, too," Sami agreed. "I only hope they like Franklin half as much."

Vin coughed a bit, but only grinned.

Eighteen

Sami managed to keep the meeting
between Franklin and her family merci-
fully brief, by arriving at 7:15—giving
them less than twenty minutes to meet,
greet, and say good-bye. She felt slightly
guilty about blowing off Celia that way,
but she could already see that Franklin was
uncomfortable with her father's questions
about whether photography was Franklin's
job or just his hobby.

They both breathed a heavy sigh of
relief as they stepped out into the New
York night and hailed a cab to take them to
the Metropolitan Museum of Art for the
benefit.

"Well, they're all you said . . . and more," Franklin said as he got into the cab beside Sami.

"I know," Sami agreed. "Hopelessly down home."

"Well, it has a certain charm," Franklin said.

Sami sat up excitedly. "You really think so?"

Franklin nodded. "They're very Martha Stewart."

"My dad has actually tried some of her recipes," Sami answered, unaware of the wry tone in his voice. "They were pretty good, too."

"Well, she still has lots of fans. There's a whole country of them out there," Franklin said.

"It's hard to remember that when you live here," Sami mused.

"I know," Franklin agreed. "That's why I've always felt Manhattan should secede from the Union."

They giggled in a conspiratorial way, as only two New Yorkers could. But there was something tentative in Sami's tone. Franklin had made jokes like that before and Sami had always found them funny. Somehow, tonight, she felt slightly disloyal as she laughed.

As the taxi pulled up in front of the museum entrance, Franklin pulled a small mirror from his jacket and checked his hair. When he was satisfied with what he saw, he placed the mirror back in his pocket, paid the driver, and hopped out to hold open the door for Sami.

"Well, the paparazzi are out in full force tonight," he said with the same bored, slightly annoyed tone Sami had heard some celebrities use at the Year in Fashion Awards show. "We may as well get it over with."

Sami shrugged. "They won't be bothering us, anyway," she assured him. "They're looking for the stars."

For a moment, Franklin looked as though he'd been punched. Then he gathered his thoughts and stood just a little straighter. "Are you kidding?" he said. "You're Sami Granger. And I'm Franklin Beane. Haven't you heard? We're the next generation of fashion royalty."

Sami smiled and began to laugh.

The really funny thing was, Franklin wasn't laughing at all. "Come on, Sami," he urged her as they walked toward the large tent that had been set up as an entranceway for invited guests. "And stop laughing. You don't want to wind up in tomorrow's paper with your eyes all squinty and the inside of your mouth showing."

Sami had never been inside the Metropolitan Museum of Art before. She'd always wanted to go, but things had gotten so busy that she hadn't had the chance. She wanted to stop and look at some of the statues and pieces of art in the huge entranceway, but Franklin pulled her away. "Nothing's happening out here, baby. We've got to be where the action is."

Sami followed Franklin through the Egyptian wing of the museum, past the mummies and papyrus paintings and finally into the huge, glass-enclosed room that was home to the Temple of Dendur exhibit. Sami gasped as she entered the room. In her whole life she had never been anywhere this beautiful. The temple itself was a small ancient stone structure that had been transported from Egypt and reconstructed in the center of the room. At the moment, carefully placed lights bathed the temple and the palm trees surrounding it in a rainbow of colors. A band played on a stage in the front of the room, and waiters walked purposefully throughout, carrying silver trays with magnificently prepared hors d'oeuvres.

"Caviar?" a waitress asked as she stopped and held out a tray of small crackers with a black topping on them.

Sami's eyes lit up. "I've always wanted to try caviar."

"You've never had it?" Franklin asked, amazed. "Oh, then, you have to!" He picked up a small cracker with a thin layer of fish eggs spread over it and popped it into Sami's mouth. It was a romantic display, something like a groom giving his bride a piece of wedding cake.

But the caviar didn't taste at all like cake. It was salty, fishy, and basically just awful. The flavor was so overwhelming that Sami forgot herself . She spit as hard as she could, desperate to get rid of the taste. The fish eggs flew out of Sami's mouth, and landed on the back of the dress of a woman standing in front of her.

"Oh, God," Sami cried out, embarrassed.

Franklin quickly dragged her across the room and away from the woman with the fish egg-stained dress. "Don't worry," he said, anxious to have Sami regain her composure before someone got suspicious. "She doesn't have eyes in the back of her head. She won't know a thing until she gets home tonight."

"But that dress must be worth at least five thousand dollars! It's an original Versace!"

"And now that woman has a touch of original Sami Granger artwork to go with it," Franklin teased. "Lucky her. A few years and she'll want to have it framed and insured."

"Artwork!"

"Sure." Franklin laughed. "Have you seen some of the things in the modern art wing? They don't look any different than that caviar stain. Now relax. Look happy. Smile."

"But that really was awful," she insisted to Franklin. "So salty. Now I'm terribly thirsty."

Franklin looked over at the bar. Real estate mogul Donald Trump was standing nearby, chatting with former New York mayor Rudy Giuliani. "I'll get you something to drink," Franklin volunteered. "Why don't you go over to the buffet and have some fruit? That'll get the fishy taste out of your mouth."

"Good idea," Sami agreed.

"What's your poison?" Franklin asked her.

"Oh, I'll just have an iced tea or something," Sami replied.

While Franklin chatted up Rudy and the Donald, Sami piled melon and grapes onto a small china plate. As she made her way down the cold buffet line, a tall, leggy woman with long blond hair stepped up beside her. "Aren't you Sami Granger?" she asked her.

Sami nodded and studied the woman's face. She didn't look familiar, but it was obvious that they must have met somewhere before, since the woman had so clearly recognized Sami. So where had they met? Was this woman one of Lola's customers? Sami doubted it. She also was pretty sure that this person wasn't the type to eat the lunch special at Hunan Garden or Pizza Piazza. "I'm sorry," Sami said finally, giving up on trying to place this woman. "I . . . well, this is so embarrassing, but I don't recall—"

"Oh, we've never met," the woman assured her. "But I'm a huge fan of your designs. I'm Lauren Madison. I know it's not right to talk business at these events, but I'm actually a buyer for Bergman Taylor and I'd like to talk to you about setting up a small boutique for your designs in our store." She slipped Sami her business card. "I suppose you've had oodles of offers, but I think there's a certain cachet to selling exclusively with us."

"Well, I could never do that. Sell exclusively, I mean. I've been working at Beneath the Sheets and—"

"Oh, that charming little downtown place," Lauren said. "I've heard of it. Anyway, I'd love to chat with you about doing something with Bergman's. Do give me a call, won't you?"

Lauren turned and walked off, refusing to give Sami a chance to say no. Sami was standing there, stunned, looking at the card in her hand, when Franklin walked up, drink in hand. "Thank you," Sami said, taking the iced tea from him. "You wouldn't believe what just happened. A buyer from Bergman Taylor just approached me!"

"What's not to believe?" Franklin asked. "I told you, baby, we're on the rise." He held out his glass. "To us," he toasted.

"To us," Sami agreed, clinking glasses. "Boy, am I thirsty." She took a huge sip of the iced tea and then placed the glass down on a nearby table.

"Let's dance," Franklin suggested, taking her around the waist and pulling her out onto the floor.

Franklin wasn't a practiced dancer, and his movements weren't always easy for Sami to follow. Still, she felt confident, even buoyant, as she danced in his arms. His own overwhelming self-confidence was obviously contagious. She smiled brightly into Franklin's eyes. He smiled back at her—just in time for their grins to be captured by one of the paparazzi.

"It's getting hot in here," she said as

they walked off the dance floor when the band took their break.

"How about another iced tea?" Franklin suggested.

"Perfect," Sami replied.

"You sit down. I'll be right back with the drinks."

Sami sank into the plush chair that had been set up near the glass wall overlooking Central Park. As she watched the people around her chat and laugh, she suddenly felt like an outsider; an impostor who didn't really belong. A roving photographer, walking toward her with his camera in hand, apparently didn't agree.

Franklin spotted the photographer focusing his attention on Sami. Within seconds, he was by her side, handing her a tall glass of iced tea.

"How about a picture, Ms. Granger?" the photographer asked.

Sami looked up at him, surprised. "You want a picture of me?"

"Of course he does, honey," Franklin said, leaning down and draping his arm around her. He looked up at the photographer. "I keep telling her she's a star. But she's so modest."

The photographer snapped the picture. "Hi, Franklin," he said. "Haven't seen you in a while."

"Well, I'm strictly doing fashion work and covers now, Jake," Franklin answered. "All by appointment. I'll leave the paparazzi work to you. It's too cutthroat for my taste."

"You used to be part of the paparazzi?" Sami asked him, surprised. She'd only known him as a fashion photographer.

"Now he's apparently on the other side of the velvet rope," Jake said.

"The view's better from here," Franklin assured him.

Jake turned his attention to Sami. "Nice meeting you, Ms. Granger. I'm sure we'll see each other again."

"I hope so," Sami replied.

"I'm sorry you had to deal with that," Franklin said soothingly after Jake walked away. "I tried to run over and shoo him away, but . . ."

Sami shook her head. "It was fine." She took a sip of her tea.

"Say, I just heard someone say that Lil' Liya just arrived. She's talking to a few friends in the main hall. Want to stop over and say hello?" Franklin suggested.

"You know her?" Sami asked incredulously. Franklin didn't seem the type to hang out with rap singers.

"We've traveled in similar circles," he replied, avoiding a direct answer. He took her by the hand. "Come on, the band's still on break, anyway."

Sami followed Franklin's lead. But before they could even move ten feet, a broad-shouldered young man with sandy blond hair made his way across the floor toward them. "Sami!" he called in his familiar deep voice.

"Bruce Jamison," Sami growled angrily.

Franklin tried to move Sami out of Bruce's path, but it was no use. Bruce was determined to speak to her. And as Sami had learned the hard way, Bruce Jamison usually got what he wanted.

"I just wanted to say congratulations," Bruce greeted her. "I've been seeing your name everywhere."

"Well, I haven't seen yours anywhere," Sami hissed.

"I've been working on a few new ideas,

but nothing's set in stone yet," Bruce replied easily.

"You mean you haven't stolen anyone else's ideas yet," Sami replied loudly.

Bruce looked around nervously. "Oh, can't we put the past behind us?" he asked. "You've had your successes, I've had mine—"

"We've both certainly had success with *my* work," Sami corrected him.

"Well, we do have similar styles," Bruce said quickly. "That's why I was thinking that maybe you and I should get together and brainstorm a bit. Maybe collaborate on a line?"

Suddenly all the resentment Sami had buried deep in her subconscious bubbled furiously back to the surface. A flood of pure adrenaline surged through her body. "Collaborate on this!" she shouted as she pulled back her fist and slammed Bruce right in the mouth.

He went flying backward, and landed with a thud on the ground. "You knocked my tooth out!" He grabbed his mouth and shrieked with pain.

Sami didn't say a word. She simply turned and left the room.

Franklin had offered to accompany Sami back to her apartment, but she'd begged off. Sami had heard a distinct lack of sincerity in his voice. It was obvious he wanted to stay, and she had to agree that there was no reason for Franklin to leave the party so early. She could handle herself just fine without him. Sami Granger didn't need anyone.

As the driver made his way downtown toward Sami's apartment, she quietly prayed that Rain was already asleep. She didn't really feel like talking at the moment. She just wanted to crawl into bed. The evening had been a disaster. The only good thing about it was that it was over. At least nothing else horribly embarrassing could happen to her tonight.

Or could it?

As Sami climbed the stairs to her apartment, she heard the sound of men's laughter ringing through the hallway. It seemed to be coming from Vin's apartment. The first voice she recognized belonged to her brother, Al.

"You should've seen little Sami holding this huge bouquet of weeds," he was saying. "She was so proud—until we told her they were poison ivy. Oh, man! That kid was covered in calamine lotion for *days*. I can't believe she never told you that story. It's a family classic."

"She's probably gotten too citified to tell a tale like that one," Sami heard her dad say. "It's not *dignified* enough."

Sami stood in the hallway outside Vin's apartment, listening to the three men laugh together. They sounded warm and comfortable as they spoke in voices slightly slurred by one too many beers. It reminded Sami of nights in her father's coffee shop— after hours, when Mac and his friends would sit around and tell their tall tales until late.

"She's had some pretty undignified moments here, too," Vin informed him glee- fully. "You know that big wooden column in her bathroom? I built that a few days ago. There's a heating pole underneath. Sami backed into it getting out of the shower. Burned her good. She couldn't sit down for three days!" The men laughed again.

Sami winced, remembering that acci- dent from the early days of the fall, when the heat first went on in the apartment. *Who leaves heating poles exposed like that?* "Okay, that's enough," she announced, bursting into the apartment. "What's this? Bust on Sami night?"

Vin stood and walked over to her. "They're just telling me what you were like as a kid. Sounds like you were pretty adorable. I wish I could've seen some of those snow people with olive necklaces and mophead wigs you built."

"Oh, that's nothing," Mac laughed. "How 'bout the time you climbed the big tree in the yard trying to rescue your cat Smoky?" He turned to Vin. "Sami got all the way to the top branch—higher than the house, even," he boasted. "Smoky took one look at her and ran down to the ground!"

"Unfortunately, Sami was too afraid to climb down after her!" Al guffawed. "We had to call the fire department. They brought a ladder to get her down!"

"Now there's a story for Page Six," Vin teased. "'What up-and-coming fashion diva got her start climbing the ladder of success chasing a cat?'"

Sami scowled at him, but she wasn't really angry. Actually, after the evening she'd just had she needed a couple of good laughs, like the kind she and Celia used to share during their all-night talks. "Where's Celia?" she asked.

"She was kinda tired, so she went back to the hotel and went to bed," Al explained. "But Vin invited us up here for a few beers. And then Rain suggested we come in and see where the great Sami Granger hangs her hat these days. Nice to see you still don't make your bed." The men all laughed again.

"So you're all sitting here talking about me without Celia to defend me?"

Mac looked at his daughter in her expensive evening gown, carefully styled updo, and dramatic makeup. "Are you so sure she would?" he asked her pointedly.

Sami sighed. He sounded just like he had in Elk Lake. His tone knocked her back to reality. So much for the warm memories of life in Elk Lake. Now she remembered why she'd left in the first place—for the same reasons she was anxious to get out of Vin's apartment now.

"I've got to get to bed," she told them. "I have two appointments in the morning."

"I thought you were spending tomorrow with us," Al said.

"I am," Sami assured him. "It's just two appointments. I'll meet you guys at the hotel around noon."

"Maybe we'd better meetcha in the lobby, Sam," Al teased. "We're on the fifteenth floor. You can get up there, but we might have to call the fire department to getcha down!"

The men collapsed into a fit of mutual laughter as Sami left the apartment, slamming the door behind her.

Nineteen

Sami stumbled into Beneath the Sheets the next morning feeling extremely grumpy. She had a horrible headache from lack of sleep—*what was I thinking drinking all that caffeine at night?* She was in no mood for any questions. She just wanted to finish up a few designs, turn them over to the two seamstresses she and Lola had recently hired, and go home to clean up before having to drag her family to every tourist site in the *Guide to New York*.

The bells ringing above the doorway echoed through her head as she walked into the shop. She mumbled angrily to herself as she rubbed her aching brow.

"Sounds like you had quite a night," Lola said from behind her copy of the *New York Courier.*

"You wouldn't believe me if I told you," Sami moaned.

"Try me," Lola said, leaning forward with a playful grin. "I hear you pack quite a punch." She turned the paper around so Sami could see the headline on Page Six.

FASHION WORLD'S ICE PRINCESS ON FIRE!

Below the headline was a huge picture of Sami slugging Bruce Jamison, with a surprised—but perfectly coiffed—Franklin by her side. It was accompanied by a small article.

> Lingerie design darlin' Sami Granger caused quite a stir last night at the benefit for the Metropolitan Museum of Art's costume collection. Amid rumors and accusations that fallen star designer Bruce Jamison had stolen her designs for his last, great collection,

Sami Granger gave Jamison a little bit of the down-home justice she learned in her hometown of Elk Lake. Seems Jesse Ventura's not the only champion fighter from Minnesota.

"Oh, no!" Sami exclaimed. "This is awful!"

"What?" Lola said. "It was time that scum got what was coming to him."

"Did you read this?" Sami asked. "It makes me seem like some country bumpkin from Mayberry or something."

"That's ridiculous," Lola said, laughing. "Don't you watch reruns on TV? Mayberry was in the South. This article very plainly states that you're an ice princess from Minnesota."

Sami shot her a look.

"All right, if you can't see the good in all this, it's not my problem," Lola said, and shrugged.

"'Good'? What good could possibly come of this?"

"Just the end of Bruce Jamison's short-lived and unearned career success," Lola suggested.

Sami jumped slightly as the phone rang. "Why is that thing turned up so loud?" she moaned, clutching her head.

Nico answered the phone. "Beneath the Sheets. How may I help you?" she asked. Then she pumped her hand triumphantly in the air.

"It's about time she got that right," Lola whispered to Sami. "Folks were beginning to think we ran some other kind of business out of this place."

"It's for you," Nico said, holding out the phone. "Vin."

Sami took the phone from Nico. "Hello?"

"Hey, slugger!" he greeted her.

"Very funny," she moaned.

"I think it's amazing," Vin said. "I wish I'd been there to see you do that! How come you didn't tell us last night about your triumph?"

"I think you heard enough tales of Country Sami last night," she replied curtly. "I didn't need to add any reports of my 'down-home justice' to the pot."

Vin laughed. "Oh, come on. I'll bet it felt great to deck that jerk!"

Sami couldn't deny it, but she didn't want to give him the satisfaction of agreeing, either.

"Okay, the real reason I called was to warn you," Vin said finally. "I think I may have given your brother and your father the address of Beneath the Sheets."

Sami gasped. "You *think*?" she demanded.

"It's hard to tell. We talked about a lot of things, so I might have inadvertently told them the block and the cross street."

"Oh Vin, you didn't. They're going to come here, I know it!"

"So what?"

Sami looked toward the door. A woman with tattoos running up and down her arms and a bright blue Mohawk had just entered the store. She walked right over to a selection of garter belts and began to examine them. "So what?" she demanded. "So what? You've met my dad—he's going to have a fit when he sees this place."

"I repeat, so what?" Vin asked. "You're a grown-up. Start acting like one. Stop hiding and sneaking off into the night like a kid. Confront your father. Tell him you're still his daughter, but the terms of the relationship have changed."

"Easy for you to say," Sami replied. "You never moved any farther than across the Brooklyn Bridge."

"You think my mother was overjoyed when I dropped out of college and went into a carpentry apprenticeship? She wanted me to be an accountant."

"Oh no, not you!" Sami exclaimed. She had a hard time imagining Vin in a suit and tie at some big firm on Wall Street.

"Oh yes," Vin said. "But I stood firm and did what was best for me, not her. Now you've got to do the same thing."

Sami thought for a moment. "Okay, could you come over here with them, though? That way I can have an ally."

"No way," Vin said.

"But—"

"Look, Sami, you know if I thought you needed me I'd be there in a heartbeat. But you don't need me for this. You have to do this one on your own."

Sami spent the rest of the morning in the back office, where she was sketching, or wasting perfectly good sheets of paper, she thought as she surveyed the discarded pages on the floor around her.

Finally, her worst fears were realized. The door opened, and the bells above signaled the arrival of the Grangers from Elk Lake, Minnesota.

"I know who you are," Lola greeted them, jumping up from behind the counter and extending her hand. "You're Sami's family. I'd have known you anywhere. You're exactly as she described you."

Mac ignored Lola's hand and looked around at the more "private" merchandise that was displayed behind the counter. "Well, this isn't exactly the way Sami described her workplace," he said disdainfully.

"Oh, it was much worse than this before she started here," Lola informed him. "Your daughter's added a lot of class to this place."

"Really?" he said. "Where?"

"Hi, everyone!" Sami shouted, running over to her family in an attempt to keep Lola from telling her father what she was so obviously thinking. "What a surprise."

"Hi, Sami," Celia greeted her. "We were kind of hoping you could get off a little early today."

"Sami doesn't need permission to take off," Lola explained to Celia. "She's a full partner, her own boss."

For a moment, Sami thought Mac looked impressed. But then his glance turned to two women examining a display of edible underwear. The women could feel his stare beating down on them. They dropped the underwear and scurried out of the shop.

"I can give the designs you've already done to the seamstresses, Sami. Get them started. In the meantime, why don't you get these guys out of here . . . I mean, get them a good lunch? How about taking them over to Tandoori Heaven?" Lola suggested quickly, trying to avoid losing any more sales that day.

"What's that?" Celia asked.

"Indian food," Lola replied. "Chicken and shrimp dipped in yogurt and then baked in a special oven. A little bit of heaven on earth, I swear."

"Funny, a woman like you talking about heaven . . . ," Mac began.

"I beg your pardon?"

"I just mean, you don't strike me as a religious type," Mac replied.

"There's a lot you don't know about me," Lola told him frankly.

"Lola's just full of surprises," Sami said, grabbing her coat and hurrying her family out the door.

"Well, she seems interesting," Al said as he and the other Grangers followed Sami down the block toward the Indian restaurant.

"She's great," Sami said. "And I owe her a lot. She gave me a job when I really needed one, and she's full of advice about the fashion business. She was the one who helped me hire seamstresses to do the actual sewing so I could spend more time designing. And she got me a lawyer to run the business end of things."

"A lawyer," Mac scoffed. "I've been in business for myself for thirty years and I never once needed a lawyer."

"Well, the fashion business is more complicated," Sami explained. "There's copyright laws, and employee compensa-

"tion issues and . . . anyway, here we are," she finished, leading her family into the restaurant and finding them a booth near the back.

"Wow, this smells delicious," Celia said, settling into a plush purple velvet booth and sniffing the air. "What's that spice?"

"Curry, I think. They use a lot of that here. The food is amazing. Real traditional cooking. The chef is from India."

Celia and Al seemed impressed. Mac just rolled his eyes.

"How about I order for us?" Sami asked. "They have really yummy breads for appetizers, and then we can try some chicken dishes, and maybe a shrimp dish. And Dad, I know you like lamb."

Mac sat stoically silent as his daughter confidently ordered the foreign-sounding dishes from the menu.

"Where'd you learn all that?" Celia asked as the waiter walked away.

"Oh, you just pick it up after a while." Sami shrugged. "Lola comes here or orders from here all the time."

"She's very cool," Celia offered.

"You're not kidding," Sami said excitedly. "She's like an icon in the Village. She knows everyone. And everyone knows her. They treat her with such respect and, because I work with her, they treat me that way too." Sami added for her dad's sake, "She takes care of me."

"It doesn't seem like you need anyone to take care of you," Al told her. "You sure gave it to that Bruce Jamison character last night. It was all over the news."

Sami blushed. "Oh, I wish you guys didn't have to see that. It was so embarrassing—"

"Embarrassing? Embarrassing?!" Mac glared at her. "Is that what you call standing up for yourself? Is that what you call putting a jerk like that in his place? As far as I'm concerned, last night was the first time you acted like my Sami since I got here. I was proud of you."

My Sami. She stared at him. "You were?"

"Heck, yeah," Mac answered. "But the way you're acting now, all haughty and sophisticated, ordering for us, and trying to act like that Lola character is someone worthy of respect, well, I'm not so sure. I think you'd better come home with me before you become one of these—"

"AAAAHHHH!"

Before Mac could finish his sentence, Celia let out a sharp cry. She grabbed her belly and bent over.

"Oh, my God! Ceil, are you okay?" Sami asked her.

"It hurts so much," Celia cried out.

"Shh. It's going to be all right," Al told her. But the paleness on his face let Sami knew he wasn't so sure. He reached over and grabbed a passing waiter. "Call an ambulance! I think my wife's in labor."

"Labor? But she can't be!" Sami said. "She's only seven months pregnant. She's got till January."

"Preterm labor," Al explained as he slipped an ice cube into Celia's mouth. "The doctor told us this could happen if she went on a plane this late in the pregnancy."

"But . . . Celia said she had a few more weeks," Sami murmured.

"It was still a risk," Al admitted.

"Then why fly out here?" Sami wailed,

looking at the agony on her best friend's face.

Al glared at Mac. "Because of him—"

"Al, *don't*," Celia begged in a small voice.

"No," Al told her. "It's about time Mac Granger found out what his stubbornness can do to people." Al turned to Sami. "He said he was coming out here to get you, no matter what. She didn't want you to have to face him alone. And the doctor said it was only a small chance that she could go into preterm labor."

"Al, you shouldn't have let her," Sami said, feeling extremely guilty. She knew her father wasn't the only one at fault. She'd been pretty stubborn herself, not having called him for all these months. Her father was silent beside her.

"I tried to talk her out of it, Sami, really, but she said you were best friends, and that she couldn't leave you stranded with him."

"Celia, if I had known . . . You didn't say he was mad . . . ," Sami stammered hopelessly, knowing that didn't really matter anymore.

At that moment, the ambulance workers rushed into the restaurant. They lifted Celia expertly onto a gurney and began to wheel her out into the street. "You can ride with us," one of the men told Al. "You two meet us at St. Vincent's emergency room."

As they carried Celia out of the restaurant, Mac collapsed back into the booth. His face was pasty white, and for a moment, Sami thought she was going to have to call for a second ambulance. Then a single tear slid from her father's eye and down his cheek. Sami was stunned. She'd never seen her father cry before. "What have I done?" he murmured. "What have I done?"

Sami reached over and put a tender arm around her father's shoulder. This was no time for blame, or arguments. This was the time Celia would need her family most. "It's okay, Dad," she assured him. "Everything's going to be okay."

Twenty

"We got here as soon as we could," Rain said, rushing into the hospital waiting room with Vin at her side. "How is she?"

"We don't know anything yet," Sami said. "The doctors and Al are in there with her. I'm sorry to have called, but I didn't know what else to do . . ."

Vin sat down beside Sami and took her hand. "Don't be sorry. Of course you should have called. We're the Three Musketeers, remember? You shouldn't be expected to go through this alone."

"She's not alone," Mac said suddenly. "She's with her *family*."

"Of course, sir," Vin said. "I just meant . . ."

Mac sighed. "Oh no, I'm sorry. I know what you meant. I'm glad my little Sami has such a good man in her life. And I'm glad it's you here instead of that long-haired good-for-nothin' Franklin Beane."

Sami thought about that for a moment. How strange that it had never occurred to her to call Franklin. When she needed someone—really needed someone—it was Vin she turned to. In fact, it had always been Vin. She took his hand and squeezed it tightly. Vin squeezed back and looked knowingly into her eyes. He understood without a word.

Mac stood up and offered Rain his seat. She refused, plopping down onto the floor instead. "And I'm glad she has a friend like you," Mac continued. "With Celia so far away, Sami needs a good girlfriend."

Sami heaved a heavy sigh. "Some friend I am. Celia risked her baby's life—and maybe her own—to help me out, and what do I do? I didn't even make time to see her. I was too busy running to *benefits* and meeting with *clients*." The words sounded strange in her mouth.

"You didn't know she was in any danger. She didn't tell you that she could have gone into labor," Mac began.

"She knew I'd tell her not to come, and she wanted to be here for me. She's a real friend. Not a jerk like me."

"You're not a jerk," Rain assured her.

"Yeah, well, I'm on my way to being one." Sami turned to her father. "You were right, Dad. The city's a lousy place. It turns people into monsters. Ever since I moved here I've done nothing but think about myself. I don't like the person I'm becoming." She took a deep breath, recognizing the importance of what she was about to say. "I'm coming home. As soon as Celia's ready to fly, I'm going home with her."

Mac looked Sami in the eye. "No, you're not," he said simply.

"What?" Sami's voice scaled up with surprise. That was not at all the response she expected from her father.

Mac put his arm around his daughter. "You know, a few days ago I would have done anything to hear you say that. But now . . ." He looked toward the closed hospital room door. "My selfishness and need to have things my way have hurt too many people. I won't ruin any more lives, Sami. This is where you belong. You have a life here. It may not be the life I'd planned for you, but it's yours. And you've got good friends. You're a good judge of people—those Franklin and Bruce characters aside. I have to trust you. Maybe if I'd trusted your mother more, given her a chance to chase her dreams, she never would have had to leave."

"But, Dad—"

"No buts about it, Sami. You're welcome to come visit—stay a month or two at a time. But Elk Lake isn't big enough for you." He turned to Vin. "I'm counting on you to make sure she doesn't get too citified," he said.

"Don't worry, sir. The minute she gets out of hand, I'll remind her about that poison ivy story, or maybe ask her to climb a tree." Vin leaned over and kissed Sami gently on the forehead. She leaned into his big, strong arms and stayed there, feeling safe.

For a long while, no one said a word. They were all focused on the door to the examining room. Every time a nurse or orderly went through the door, they could catch a glimpse of where Celia lay on the big table surrounded by strange doctors and bright lights.

"She must be petrified," Sami said quietly.

"She's okay, she's got Al there," Vin assured her. Sami nodded and rubbed her cheek against his. She was suddenly well aware of how important having someone by your side could be. *Celia was right*.

Al finally emerged from the examination room. His shirt was wet with sweat and his hair was a mess, but he looked relieved.

"Is Celia okay?" Sami asked, leaping up from her seat.

"How about the baby, son?" Mac added.

Al took a sip of water from a nearby fountain. "Everyone's okay. It wasn't really preterm labor. It was something called a Braxton-Hicks contraction. They can start up around now. Usually it's just the belly tightening up a bit, but sometimes they can really hurt. And Celia's had such a tough time of it up till now, that I guess we both got a little scared. Anyhow, they're going to keep her here, just overnight for observation, and then"——he turned to Sami—"I think we're going to have to go home early, kiddo. I want Celia close to her doctor, just in case."

Sami nodded. "You should be home. Can I see her now?"

"She's been asking for you."

Sami raced for the door. She took a deep breath and then entered the room.

Celia was propped up on a gurney, dressed in one of those horrible hospital gowns. But the color had returned to her face, and she looked more like her old self.

"What, you didn't think New York was exciting enough?" Sami asked her, trying to sound light and breezy, although that was far from how she felt. "You had to add a little of your own thrills to this trip?"

"I kind of overreacted," Celia admitted.

"No way," Sami said, shaking her head. "You were scared, and far from home."

"People do weird stuff when they're scared and far from home, huh?" Celia asked pointedly.

Sami blushed. "I've kind of been making a jerk of myself over the past few months,

313

a jerk of myself over the past few months, haven't I?"

"You said it, I didn't." Celia smiled. "Still, it's good to hear it out loud."

"I've missed you, I really have," Sami told her. "I told Dad I want to come home and be there with you, but he won't let me. Which is okay, I think, because I don't know if I can leave Vin and—"

"Vin, huh?" Celia said. "Well, it's about time."

"About time?"

"Sami, you've been telling me about your best friend Vin since you moved here. I knew you were crazy about him, but you sure were dense."

Sami laughed. "You always knew me better than I knew myself. Which is why I want to come home—"

"Oh no, you don't," Celia warned. "You're not giving up on your half of the bargain. You were supposed to become famous so I could be the best friend of a celeb, and so my daughter could have an aunt she could really brag about on Career Day. And there's no way you could do that in Elk Lake."

Sami shrugged. "I guess," she said slowly.

"Besides, there's such a thing as airplanes, you know. You could take a trip or two. You don't have to be a total stranger."

Sami reached over and hugged Celia gratefully. "I won't be. I promise."

Vin was waiting for Sami as she walked out of Celia's room. "Rain took your father and Al for a cup of coffee," Vin explained quietly. He glanced toward the hospital room where Celia lay. "How is she?"

"It's going to be okay," Sami said, as much to assure herself as anything else. She looked up at him. "I'm glad you're here."

"I wouldn't be anywhere else," he said softly, pulling her close.

Sami looked into his eyes. He stared back at her, his expression filled with questions. There was only one way for Sami to give him the answers he needed. She reached up and kissed him.

"I've got to meet some friends in about twenty minutes," Rain announced as she, Sami, and Vin left the hospital together late that night. "You'll have to soldier on without me."

Sami gave her roommate a grateful smile. It was obvious that Rain had sensed the change in the dynamic between the Three Musketeers, and she was giving Sami and Vin time to sort things out.

The November night was cool. Vin reached over to put his arm around Sami as if to protect her from the cold night air as they walked home. Sami laughed lightly to herself—she was, after all, a Minnesota girl. She was used to the cold.

What she *wasn't* used to was being with Vin, at least not in this way. As they reached the doorway to their building, she felt her heart pounding wildly. *This is silly,* she tried to tell herself. After all, she and Vin had crossed this threshold a thousand times together, after trips to the park or late-night pizza runs.

But this was different, and they both knew it. Once Sami entered Vin's apartment tonight, nothing would ever be the same.

"Um, I'm sorry about the mess," Vin apologized as he fumbled with the keys to his apartment. "Your call caught me off guard."

"It can't be any messier than my room," Sami said, keeping the small talk going. "I have more clothes on my bed than in my closet."

Vin nodded, and once again they slipped into an abyss of uncomfortable silence. Sami sat gingerly on the couch, and Vin sat down beside her, taking care to be close but not so close as to make her uncomfortable.

Sami's heart beat faster, and she could feel a hot red blush rising up onto her cheeks. She hoped Vin couldn't tell just how nervous she was, but deep down she was sure he could. There was no way she could keep anything from him: Vin always knew what she was thinking. He'd proven it that night when they were dancing at Lincoln Center, and probably a million times since then. There was no doubt in her mind that Vin could tell how badly she wanted him. *Needed him.* There was no sense in trying to hide it. Slowly, tentatively, she reached over and gently ran her finger across his hand.

The effect was explosive. Vin leaned over and kissed her, gently at first, as if he were afraid she would break. Sami pulled him closer to her, letting him know that she wanted this as much as he did. Vin moved his lips gently down her face, kissing her neck and shoulders passionately as he gently stroked her hair and the side of her cheek. Sami breathed heavily, overcome with joy and excitement. She'd loved Vin from the moment she'd met him. She had just been too blind to see it. Now, here in his apartment, on a cold November night, all of the months of love for Vin poured out of her in one long, passionate kiss. She used her lips to let him know that, now and forever, her heart belonged to him.

Epilogue

Celia entered the models' dressing room and searched for Sami. She finally spotted her kneeling down beside one of the models, giving her nightshirt one last stitch. "There you are," Celia said. "I've been looking everywhere for you."

Sami leaped up and squeezed her newly svelte best chum. "You look amazing," Sami said. "I love that suit. It's so chic."

"Well, I'm in the fashion business now," Celia reminded her. "How else would you like the manager of the Elk Lake offices of Sami Granger Designs to look?"

"I wouldn't change a thing," Sami assured her. "Where's Alana?"

"With her proud poppa, of course," Celia said. "Are you sure you want her here? She could cry at any moment. She's only two years old, you know."

"Hard to believe," Sami murmured. "Of course I want her here. I need my family around today. Where's Dad?"

"He's already seated, right next to Lola. They're exchanging battle stories from the nineteen sixties. Personally, I think they're both full of it, but . . ."

"As long as they're enjoying themselves." Sami laughed. "Whoever thought that they would become friends?"

"I think it was that trip Lola made with you when you opened the Elk Lake office. She and Mac went off during that party and we didn't see them for *hours*," Celia said, giggling.

Sami laughed, remembering. "Celia, I'm so glad you agreed to run things in Elk Lake when I'm not there," she said. "I feel so much better knowing it's in your hands."

"Are you kidding?" Celia said. "I'm having a blast. And everyone in town thinks of you as some sort of hero. Putting your headquarters in Elk Lake has given lots of people jobs, you know. And adding that day care center was a stroke of genius. I had no idea how many moms wanted to work if they could find a way to be close to their kids."

"Well, this wise woman I know once told me that all the success in the world wasn't worth anything if you couldn't share it with family," Sami admitted.

Celia laughed. "Whoever could that be?"

"Gee, I wonder."

"Anyway, you've put Elk Lake on the map—just like you promised."

"Let's hope it's still that way after this show," Sami said worriedly.

"Nervous?" Celia asked.

Sami nodded. "My first fashion show. I can't believe it."

"Believe it," Celia said. "*Enjoy* it." She gave Sami a hug. "I've got to sit down. See you after the show."

Sami started to say something, but then she heard her name. "Sami, there's a rip in this sleeve," one of the models cried out.

"Coming," Sami called, running toward a girl in a blue nightshirt.

"Five minutes," the stage manager called into the dressing room.

"Oh God," Sami gasped, suddenly finding it hard to catch her breath.

Rain rushed to her side. "You okay, boss?" she asked.

Sami looked at her friend. She looked adorable in her pink-and-red pinstripe nightshirt. Her red hair hung straight and simple down her back. "You look gorgeous," she told Rain.

"You think so?" Rain asked, unsure. "The nightshirt is a piece of genius, but I still think you should've gone with a more famous model to start the show. I would have been happy just to be one of the gang."

Sami shook her head. "No way. You're the face of Sami Granger Designs. You need to start the show."

Rain nodded. "It's amazing, isn't it? When you first moved in you were a receptionist and I was serving veggie burgers at Dojo."

"Now you're in magazines and on runways," Sami told her.

"And you're not doing too shabby

either," Rain teased. "I just wish I saw you more. Ever since you moved out . . ."

"I only moved across the hall," Sami told her. "And you're over at our place all the time."

"But you're not," Rain said. "You spend almost half your time in Elk Lake."

"That's why I need you," Sami teased. "To keep an eye on Vin for me."

"He's really a great guy," Rain told her. "And he adores you. You don't need anyone to watch him."

"I know," Sami agreed. "He understands that part of me still needs to be in Elk Lake. And he's cool with that."

"Where is he, anyway?" Rain asked.

"Putting some last-minute finishing touches on his set design, I think. He's such a perfectionist."

"It's an incredible set," Rain said.

"Vin is amazing," Sami agreed.

"So are you. So am I," Rain cheered. "The Three Musketeers rule!"

"Rain, they need you at the curtain," the stage manager called out. "It's starting."

Rain gave Sami one last hug and ran toward the stage.

★

The show lasted about an hour. One by one the models walked down the runway, playfully showing off Sami's original lingerie designs. Sami had made sure they all understood that they were to smile and act joyous. She had no patience for the overblown cooler-than-thou attitude of most fashion shows. When it came time for the big finale, the curtains parted to display a giant bed with a trampoline mattress that had been specially built by Vin and his crew of stagehands. The models, all dressed in baby dolls and nightshirts, hopped up and down like kids playing on their parents' bed. It was a perfect ending for a show that demonstrated just how much fun lingerie could be.

"Okay, Sami, it's your turn," the stage manager whispered, practically pushing her onto the stage. Sami walked out slowly and stood shyly in front of the bouncing models. The lights were bright and it was hard to see, but she could tell that the audience was on its feet, giving her a standing ovation. More importantly, Sami knew that everyone she cared about was out there cheering for her. There were her Elk Lake relatives: Mac, Al, Celia, and little Alana. But Sami had come to realize that she had family in New York as well. Maybe not blood relatives, but the bonds were just as strong. Lola had a front-row seat for the event, and was as proud of Sami as any mother could be. Nico was there, too, applauding wildly and letting out a loud wolf whistle as the crowd cheered. Sami had even sent an invitation to Ella, the Très Joli representative she'd met at the Bridal Building her first day in New York. The woman probably had no idea why she'd received the card in the mail, but for Sami, it was a way of repaying an old debt.

Most importantly, Vin was in the front row, a fact that gave Sami great comfort. It was reassuring to know that, no matter how scary this day was, when it was all over she would wind up going home with Vin—a man who wanted nothing more than for her to love him as much as he loved her. And Sami did love Vin. When she had time to indulge herself with a bit of fantasy, she could actually see them married to each other and raising a brood of beautiful babies. But there was time for that. Both she and Vin were satisfied with the way things were at the moment.

It had taken Sami a long time to learn to accept both sides of herself: the small-town girl and the New York fashion designer. But she had to accept them both, because the Sami Granger she was today was a combination of the girl she had once been in Elk Lake and the woman she had become since moving to New York City. Sami wasn't willing to relinquish either one. Still, it wasn't easy combining the two. She spent a lot of time on airplanes going back and forth from Minnesota to New York. It seemed as though she was always saying good-bye or being welcomed home by someone. But as Sami stood onstage with the models who were displaying her designs and beamed into the audience where her loved ones sat, she knew she wouldn't have it any other way.

For the first time, Sami Granger felt totally and utterly complete. The varying threads of her existence had been perfectly seamed to form a single fabric—the fabric of her life.

About the Author

Nancy Krulik is the author of more than one hundred books for children and young adults. She has written biographies of many of today's major celebrities, including the *New York Times* best-selling *Leonardo DiCaprio: A Biography.* She has just completed a new book for Simon Pulse, *Love & Sk8.* Nancy lives in Manhattan with her husband, composer Daniel Burwasser, their two children, Ian and Amanda, and a crazed cocker spaniel named Pepper.